'If you like Jacqueline Wilson, then you'll love Judi Curtin!'
Primary Times

'Rising star Judi Curtin's "Alice" books celebrate friendship, humour
and loyalty.'
Sunday Independent

'Engrossing story with a real insight into the world of pre-teen girls.'
Publishing News

JUDI CURTIN grew up in Cork and now lives in Limerick where she is married with three children. She is the best-selling author of the 'Alice & Megan' series: *Alice Next Door, Alice Again, Don't Ask Alice, Alice in the Middle, Bonjour Alice* and *Alice & Megan Forever*. With Roisin Meaney, she has written *See If I Care*. She has also written three novels, *Sorry, Walter!, From Claire to Here* and *Almost Perfect*.

All About Alice:
Alice Next Door and
Alice Again

Judi Curtin

Illustrations: Woody Fox

THE O'BRIEN PRESS
DUBLIN

For Mum and Dad,
and for Dan, Brian, Ellie and Annie

This edition first published 2007 by The O'Brien Press Ltd.
First published as *Alice Next Door* (2005)
and *Alice Again* (2006) by The O'Brien Press Ltd,
12 Terenure Road East, Rathgar, Dublin 6, Ireland.
Tel: +353 1 4923333; Fax: +353 1 4922777
E-mail: books@obrien.ie
Website: www.obrien.ie
Reprinted 2009.

ISBN: 978-1-84717-051-4

British Library Cataloguing-in-Publication Data
All about Alice
1. Best friends - Juvenile fiction 2. Children's stories, English
I. Title II. Fox, Woody
823.9'2[J]

2 3 4 5 6 7 8
09 10 11 12

The O'Brien Press receives assistance from

Illustrations: Woody Fox
Layout and design: The O'Brien Press Ltd
Printing: CPI Cox & Wyman

Chapter one

Sheila Sheehan says that I'm the most beautiful girl in the world. She says my eyes are the
prettiest shade of blue she's ever seen. Sometimes
she combs my hair for me and she says it's the
silkiest hair she's ever touched in all her life.

She has to say all that stuff though. She's my
mum. It's her job.

My mum has a lot to say on every subject. Sometimes I tell her to lighten up, but she only gives me
her exasperated look, and continues anyway.

Mum says that my best friend Alice's mum is
an evil, selfish cow.

But she only says that when she thinks I'm not
listening.

It doesn't matter anyway. Alice and her mum have gone to live in Dublin. Her dad still lives next door to us, but that's not much good to me, is it? He won't want to take basketball shots with me, or to play Monopoly, or to lie on the floor of my room listening to music, and laughing at nothing.

At first, when Alice told me she was leaving, I hoped that she'd be down to see her dad at weekends. We could still be friends. That's the way it works in books anyway. Or in films – as long as they're rated PG. Real life wasn't turning out like that though. Alice's mum pulled what my mum calls her master-stroke. She enrolled Alice and her brother, Jamie, in piano classes on Saturday afternoons. That means that they can't come to Limerick at all, except at holiday time, and for long weekends. If Alice's dad wants to see her any other time, he'll have to go all the way to Dublin. It's September now, and the next long weekend isn't for weeks and weeks and weeks. Mum says not to get my hopes up too much because Veronica, (that's

Alice's mum) will probably find some reason not to send the kids to see their dad. But I have to hope. What else can I do?

And I have to face into school tomorrow. It'll be the first time ever without Alice in my class. We started together in junior infants, and have been together ever since. We were together when Alice spilt milk on her trousers and had to change into the horrible brown scratchy ones the teacher kept in the cupboard under the nature table. And everyone else thought she'd wet her knickers.

Alice never laughed at me when my mum gave me carrot sticks and broccoli for school lunch. With a bottle of water to wash it all down.

Alice was the only one who didn't tease me when I had to go to school in darned tights because Mum said it was a waste to throw them out just because of one small hole. (I said I'd skip on the organic porridge for a week and spend the savings on new tights, but Mum didn't think that was funny.)

I never laughed at Alice when her mum forgot to pack any lunch at all for her, and the teacher had to ask all the kids to share and everyone offered the worst, soggy, squashed thing in their lunchboxes. Once she had to take an egg sandwich from Tom, who hadn't washed his hands in about five hundred years. Luckily I was able to distract him while she threw it into the bin. That's what friends are for, isn't it?

*　　　*　　　*

Alice and her mum left yesterday. It had been planned for weeks though. Alice's mum said she was leaving Alice's dad because they just couldn't get on. 'Irreconcilable differences', was what she said.

My mum said that if Alice's dad got the big promotion and the new silver BMW she'd been hoping for, they'd have got on just fine. She said Alice's mum was a social climber of the highest order. She'd never be happy living in a three-bedroomed semi, and driving around in a four-year-old car.

Of course, Mum didn't think I was listening when she said all of this on the phone to my aunt Linda. She should be more careful.

Anyway, it was awful when Alice left. If it was a film, I suppose I'd have cried and hugged her and we would have promised to be friends forever. I couldn't though. Alice and I weren't huggy kind of girls. I just felt very sad.

'Bye, Al,' I said.

'Bye, Meg,' she said.

Usually there wasn't enough time to say all the things I wanted to say to Alice. Right then though, I couldn't think of anything else to say.

She looked sad too. 'Don't forget to send me lots of e-mails.'

'Oh yeah. I will. I mean I won't forget. I promise. I'll send lots of e-mails. Every day.'

Alice smiled a funny, stiff kind of smile.

'And don't forget to say "hi" to Melissa for me.'

I groaned. Melissa is the meanest girl in the world. Alice and I have both hated her since forever. Now I'd have to hate her all on my own. And that's no fun.

Alice's mum put her fancy light brown designer handbag on the front seat of the car and then she sat into the driver's seat. She turned the driving mirror towards herself and fixed her hair. Then she put on some lipstick. Imagine, putting on lipstick for a drive to Dublin. Did she think it would show up on the speed cameras?

'Come on, Alice. If we don't go soon we'll be stuck in traffic all afternoon. It'll be teatime before we get through Castletroy.'

It was Saturday, so that was a stupid thing to say. Even I knew there were never traffic jams on Saturdays. Alice didn't argue though. She just got into the car, and helped Jamie with his seat belt. Then her mum started the engine, and they drove off.

I waved until they were out of sight. That didn't take long. They live right at the top of the road and they were gone in about three and a half seconds.

Mum hugged me as we went inside, and offered to make me a fruit smoothie. As if that would help. Even a huge Coke wouldn't have made me feel better, and there was fat chance of getting one of those.

Later Mum took me shopping. We went to O'Mahony's bookshop and she bought me two new books. Then she bought me a new T-shirt, a spotty scrunchie and a comic. When she bought the comic I knew she must be feeling really sorry for me. Last time she bought me a comic was when my goldfish died. (The fish had gone a really revolting black colour, and had big warty lumps all down its back. I was glad it was dead. But luckily Mum didn't know that. And the comic more than made up for the loss of the fish.) This was different though. A year's supply of comics wouldn't have helped. No point in reading a comic on my own. Reading comics was only fun when Alice was around. She made everything more fun. Even stupid things that shouldn't have been fun at all.

When we got home, my little sister Rosie asked if she could read the comic. She's only three, and can't read anyway, but I let her. She tore two pages and I didn't even care.

Chapter two

First day in sixth class over. My last year in National School. My eighth and last time to walk into that ugly grey building at the beginning of a new school year. My first time to walk in without Alice by my side.

It was awful. There were the usual awful things – like being the only one whose books were

covered in old wallpaper instead of shiny coloured contact. And being the only one who
didn't have new markers or colouring pencils.
Mum made me root through our big box of colouring stuff for a set of pencils. I ended up with
one of every colour, but none of them matched,
and all of them were dirty-looking.

Mum didn't care. 'Everyone's pencils will be
dirty in a week. And at least you won't be con-
tributing to the piles of rubbish in our city.'

Mum has a big thing about piles of rubbish.
Every time I ask for something new she says.
'You don't even need it. It'll only end up in a big
pile of rubbish.'

Anyway, as well as all the usual bad things
about school, there was the really, really, really
bad thing of Alice not being there.

Our new teacher, Miss O'Herlihy, said we
could sit wherever we liked for the first day. That
was the worst part, I think. Melissa and all her
buddies grabbed the seats at the back and sat

there like big grinning hyenas. The boys all sat with each other as usual. The twins Ellen and Emma sat together of course, in their own exclusive little club of two. So that just left me and Jane.

Jane and I have a lot in common now. We both have no friends. Only difference is, Jane doesn't deserve them. She still tells tales, even in sixth class. And she thinks everyone except for her is 'frightfully immature'. She has her hair cut short like a boy's, and she wears a helmet when she cycles to school. I know it might save her life some day, but it's social death to be seen in a cycle helmet, and Jane doesn't even care.

We stood at the side of the room and looked at each other. I couldn't decide which was worse – sitting on my own, or sitting with Jane. In the end it didn't matter. There were only two seats left anyway, and they were together, right at the front of the class, touching Miss O'Herlihy's desk.

As I saw it, I had only two choices. I could run away and cry, or I could sit down. I decided to be brave. I slowly walked to the top of the room, and took one of the empty seats. Jane sat next to me. She took out her Barbie pencil case and began to arrange her pens on the desk. And the pencil case wasn't even a present from a mad aunt. Jane bought it herself with her pocket money. I was sure I could hear Melissa sniggering somewhere behind me. I didn't look around.

I think it's time to tell you about Melissa.

She's beautiful, in a horrible, conceited kind of way. She has shiny blonde hair, which she never ties up. She just lets it sort of float all around her face like the princesses in my old fairy-story books. When I leave my hair loose I look like a cartoon witch.

All the teachers love Melissa. She's fooled them you see. They don't know how mean she is when they aren't around. They think she's all sweet and perfect. Considering how much time the teachers spend telling us to not to judge people by their appearance, it's a bit stupid of them to have fallen for Melissa's innocent smile, and her exquisite blonde beauty.

Melissa has a secret club. The club doesn't have any rules or any passwords or anything. They think they're too cool for that kind of thing. It's just a big group of girls who all think that Melissa is the greatest thing since water yo-yos. Mostly all they do is gather around her, and admire her hair and her trendy clothes, and laugh at her jokes.

Melissa never liked Alice and me. I don't know why. Alice didn't care. And when Alice was around, I didn't care that much either. But without Alice, all the bad things seemed worse. Every time Melissa laughed, I was sure she was laughing at me. And every time one of her friends whispered to another, I was sure they were telling awful secrets about me.

After school, I walked home on my own,

missing Alice more than ever. It wasn't any fun, and for the first time ever, it felt like a very long walk.

Mum asked me how my day was, and I just said, 'fine', even though there wasn't a single fine thing about it.

I had nothing to do after school. This was time I should have been spending with Alice. I half-wished that I had homework – at least it would have been something to do. I couldn't tell Mum that I was bored though. Whenever I did that, her reaction was the same. She'd give a huge sigh, and say that she'd love the chance to be bored. Then she'd give me a long list of horrible jobs like tidying the odd-sock drawer or dusting the skirting boards.

In the end, Mum let me go on the computer, so I checked to see if there was an e-mail from Alice.

There wasn't. She was probably too busy having fun with all her fancy new Dublin friends. She was probably planning her first sleepover party. Or drawing up a list of friends to invite to the pictures, or for a pizza. My mum said Alice's mum was a great one for 'throwing money at her problems'. No chance of my mum doing that. It wouldn't have helped anyway. Even if Mum did have a personality transplant, and gave me fifty euro to take my friends out for a treat, who would I ask? There was no one. No one at all. I'd be the sad girl, all alone in the cinema, with three boxes of popcorn and five cups of Coke and no friends.

I felt like crying then. I wondered if tears would damage the computer keyboard.

Mum came in and saw me looking at the blank screen. She rubbed my head and asked if I wanted to watch television. She even let me watch *The Simpsons*, without sighing and shaking her head every few minutes. I knew then that she must be feeling really sorry for me.

And that made me feel even worse.

Chapter three

Over the next few days, I sent Alice lots of e-mails, but they all came bouncing straight back to me like stupid, unwanted boomerangs. I didn't know why. Alice was always better with computers than I was. She would have understood. But there wasn't much point in e-mailing her to ask why my e-mails weren't getting to her, was there?

Mum said I could phone Alice instead, but only on Saturday when long-distance calls are cheaper. I wonder how come she always knows that kind of thing?

School didn't improve as the week went on. But then, I hadn't really expected it to. At twelve I was too big to believe in easy solutions.

Melissa and her buddies loved being in sixth class. They sort of sailed up and down the corridors, flicking their hair and wiggling their bottoms, and all the little kids looked up to them like they were real important.

In the yard, they sat on the benches, and tossed their hair some more, and tried their best to look cool and sophisticated. Jane spent yard time reading books about boring stuff like ancient history. Ellen and Emma walked around in their own little world, as if no-one else even existed. And all the boys played football. Even the boys who hated PE played football. I suppose it's their way of being part of the gang.

Miss O' Herlihy is nice enough. For a teacher. She smiles a lot, but for some reason even the boldest kids do what she says. She was nice to me, and talked to me in a gentle, interested kind of voice. Like she really cared. I wondered if she was sorry for me because it looked like I had no friends. Sometimes I felt like telling Miss O'Herlihy that I did have a friend, but that she moved away. Then I thought that sounded really silly, so I didn't say it. Maybe she knew anyway. Maybe the other teachers told her. Maybe not though. I bet they had more interesting stuff to talk about in the staff-room. Like where to buy cheap baked beans, and quick ways to mark maths copies and stuff.

At last Saturday morning came. At eight o' clock, I went in to Mum and Dad's room.

'Can I phone Alice now? Remember you promised?'

Dad poked his head from under the covers.

'Huh. It's a bit early, isn't it? Bet her mum isn't home yet.'

Mum kicked him under the duvet, and he didn't say any more. I knew what he meant though. Dad thinks Alice's mum goes out every night, and stays out really late going to clubs and things. Still, maybe he's just jealous, because he never goes anywhere except to work and soccer matches.

Mum gave Dad a really cross look. She smiled at me.

'No darling, don't ring just yet. They might still be in bed. Wait until half nine.'

I went back to my room and waited. It seemed like a very long time. I looked at the picture of Alice and me that I kept next to my bed. It was in a 'Best Friends' frame, that we agreed was a bit babyish, but just about cute enough not to matter. Alice had one the same. I felt sure she wasn't looking at hers. She was probably planning what to wear to a party in a new friend's house. Or wondering which of her new friends to go shopping with. Maybe she had taken my picture out of the frame and replaced it with a photo of one of her new friends. Alice wasn't disloyal by nature, but she was smart. I wasn't much good to her when I lived so far away. I couldn't blame her for trying to make new friends. The thought of that made me really sad, though.

At last half past nine came. I took the portable phone into my room, and dialled the number Alice had given me.

Alice answered after only three rings. Her voice was kind of quiet.

'Hello?'

'Hi, Al. It's me, Meg. How are you?'

'Meg!' She said it in a real excited way that made me feel happy and sad at the same time.

'Meg,' she said again. 'It's great to hear from you. How's school? What's Miss O'Herlihy like? How is Melissa? How are you?'

I laughed. Alice was always in a rush to talk. Like she had too many things to say, and not enough time to say them all.

'Well. School's awful without you. I have to sit next to Jane.'

'Ouch. Poor you.'

Then I felt a bit mean.

'Well, Jane's not so bad. Just kind of boring you know. We don't have a whole lot in common, you know. Miss O'Herlihy's nice – for a teacher. Melissa was always awful anyway. And I feel awful.'

Alice spoke quietly. 'Yeah, I know. My school's OK. The teacher's nice. And the kids are too. But they all have their own friends, and I know they're only being nice to me because the teacher asked them to. They're kind of polite and friendly for a little while, and then they rush back to their old friends, looking kind of pleased with themselves for being so nice to the "new girl". My uniform is yuck. It's brown like your dad's car. And the material is all scratchy. And the tie is the colour of your old fish's skin before it died. And our apartment is kind of boring. It's all painted a kind of light creamy colour. Mum says it's minimalist. I think it looks as if the owner was too mean to buy much furniture. There's no garden. Just a balcony. When you stand on it all you can see is the car park. I hate it.'

I wasn't sure what I should say to that.

'Do you miss your dad?'

She gave a scornful kind of laugh.

'Course I do. Wouldn't you?'

Then I felt kind of stupid. What kind of a daft question was that?

There was a moment's silence, and then Al spoke again.

'Hey, Meg, look out quick. Is Dad's car there? He's coming up to see me today.'

I went into the front room and looked out of the window. Her dad's car was gone from its usual place.

'No, Al. It's gone.'

'Great, he's on his way so. He's taking me to the zoo. Mum took us there on Monday after school, but I don't think I should tell Dad that. He thinks it's going to be a big treat. I'll have to pretend to be really excited about it, which is a pain. The animals stink really badly. Almost as badly as Darren Blake's football boots.'

I giggled. 'That bad?'

'Yeah. That bad. And then, after the zoo, we're going for pizza.'

'Well,' I said. 'You love pizza. So at least that'll be a treat, won't it?'

Alice sighed. 'Not really. We've had pizza three times this week already. The delivery boy knows all our names by now., and which kinds of pizzas we like. Mum says that with all the hassle from the move, she hasn't time to be cooking as well.'

'Is your dad going to stay with you tonight?'

'No. Mum said they could be civilised, and he could sleep in Jamie's room, but Dad said no. So he's staying with our Uncle John. I wish he'd stay with us.'

I wandered back into my room and lay on my bed. 'Maybe he'll stay with you next time.' I was fairly sure he wouldn't, but didn't like to say so. I changed the subject. 'Have you fixed up your e-mail yet?'

'No, but Dad's going to connect up the

computer for me tonight.' She laughed then. 'Mum tried to connect it, but she couldn't get it to work. Then she got really mad. She threw the manual on the floor after a while. And then she said all the bad words she won't let me use. Jamie copied her, and she banned him from sweets for the rest of the day. It wasn't fair on him, but I wasn't arguing, not with the mood she was in.'

I laughed. Al was always good at telling stories. I wanted to tell her that I missed her. That things were all different now that she was gone. But I thought that might have sounded kind of stupid. Only girls on the telly got away with saying that kind of thing.

So I told her about Rosie's new back tooth, and Mum's new haircut, and how Dad asked if the hairdresser was cross with her, and how they rowed for twenty minutes afterwards.

After a while, Mum tapped on the door and came into my room. She looked like she was still in a bad mood. She pointed to her watch. I held up one finger to show I wanted to talk for one more minute. She nodded and went back out.

'I have to go soon, Al. When are you coming to Limerick? Will your mum let you come down soon?'

Alice made a sad kind of sighing noise.

'I don't think so. She says after all she's paid up front for my music lessons, I'm only allowed to miss one if I'm nearly dead. I don't know if I'll ever be back again.'

I felt like crying, but that would have been too pathetic, so I very quickly said

'Bye, Al. Talk to you next week.'

Then I hung up.

I lay on my bed and looked at the ceiling. I could see the glow-in-the-dark stickers that Alice had helped me stick up. She had thought of a very clever trick using a sweeping brush and a tiny piece of Blu-Tak. Alice always had great ideas. I really missed her.

I cried for a little while, but it didn't make me

feel any better, so I got dressed and went downstairs for breakfast.

It was porridge.

As if I didn't feel quite bad enough already.

Chapter four

On Monday I got an e-mail from Alice. I was really excited. It was the first one I ever got. (Not counting all the ones I got telling me my messages to her were undelivered.) I scrolled really quickly through it, reading as fast as I could.

```
Dear Meg,
   This is my first e-mail. I
hope you get it. I had an ok
weekend. Dad took me and Jamie
lots of places. He never found
```

out that we'd been to the zoo
already. I had bribed Jamie
with a whole packet of Star-
burst, just in case. I knew it
would work because as you know,
Jamie would do anything for
sweets. Dad was kind of sad
though. Mum was kind of bubbly,
and nice to Dad, but it didn't
help. Actually, I think that
made it worse. Yesterday when
Dad was going away, Jamie was
crying. I felt like crying too,
but I thought that would make
Dad sadder, so I pretended to
be happy. Afterwards I thought
he might have been a bit
insulted so next week I might
try a kind of brave, sad look.
When Dad was gone, Mum gave
Jamie and me a big bag of
sweets each. I know that's what
happens in films. She's trying

to make it up to us because now
we're kids from a broken home.
She must be mad if she thinks a
bag of sweets will make up for
being away from home, and from
Dad and from you. I'm a bit old
to be so easily fooled. I don't
think Jamie even fell for it.
School was a bit better today.
A girl called Sophie shared her
crisps with me, and we chatted
in the yard. Have to go now.
Tea's ready. It's pizza
(again!!!!). I'll ring you on
Saturday.
Al xxx

I was all excited. When I'd finished reading it, I
read it again a bit more slowly. Mum was nice
and even stopped peeling the potatoes to show
me how to reply. When she was safely back in the
kitchen, this is what I wrote.

Dear Al

This is my first e-mail too. Well, the first one you might actually get. My weekend was real boring. Yesterday Dad made us go to Cratloe for a real long walk. It was pouring rain, but Dad just kept on saying 'a bit of drizzle never hurt anyone, sure isn't your skin waterproof?' That really annoyed me. We went off the track and got lost. Mum got cross and said 'what if I had high heels on?' Dad laughed and said she hadn't worn high heels since the day she got married. Mum pretended to be even crosser, but I knew she wasn't. Then they got all smoochy, (yuck) and I had to wheel Rosie's buggy. That was very

hard because the path was all
bumpy. In the end Dad had to
take over and Mum walked with
me. She kept talking about
feelings and stuff, so I ran
after Dad and pretended I
wanted to look for conkers. We
didn't find any, but at least
it kept Mum off my back. We had
pancakes for tea (yum). School
today was still awful. Melissa
is as smug as ever. Can't think
of any more to write. Looking
forward to talking to you on
Saturday.

Meg

At dinnertime, Mum kept going on to Dad
about the e-mails. You'd think I'd discovered a
cure for cancer or something.

'Isn't it great, Donal? Megan and Alice are
e-mailing each other. Isn't that a grand way of

keeping in touch? Technology's great all the same, isn't it?'

Dad just kept on nodding. I was really cross, though. What good were e-mails? I wanted a real friend. One I could see, and mess around with and laugh with. Not one who existed only on a white screen, and through a telephone. What kind of a friend was that?

I felt like shouting all that out to Mum, when she kept on about the wonders of new technology and stuff, but I didn't. I hadn't been Mum's daughter for twelve years for nothing. I knew she'd be sympathetic, but then I'd be rewarded with hours of speeches about feelings and stuff. It wasn't worth it.

So I tidied up after the dinner, and played with Rosie and waited for bedtime.

When Mum came to tuck me in, I had a great idea.

'Mum, you know how you think technology is so great?'

She looked at me suspiciously.

'Yes.'

'Well, if I had a mobile phone, I could text Alice whenever I liked. It would be a good use of technology, don't you think?'

Mum laughed. '

A good use of my money, you mean. Come on Megan. You know I don't like mobile phones. We still don't know what they do to your brain. A lot of people might be very sorry in a few years time. Very sorry indeed. I think you'd better just stick to the landline, and the computer.'

She kissed me, and went out of the room.

I snuggled under the blankets, and sighed. I love my mum, but she's such a dinosaur it's totally embarrassing. I was sure I lived in the most backward house in Ireland. If a huge volcano, like the one in Pompeii, erupted in our back garden, and covered our house with lava, it would surely fool the archaeologists in a million years time. They'd have awful trouble trying to decide when it happened.

They'd scrunch up their faces.

'Hmm. Carbon dating says twenty-first century, and we have found a computer, but that couldn't be right.'

The others would chorus.

'No microwave oven.'

'No mobile phones.'

'No tumble drier.'

'No pizza packets.'

'No Playstation.'

'No video.'

And then they'd go home and write their papers and decide we lived in the 1950s or some ancient time like that.

It's just not fair.

Chapter five

I give out a lot about my mum. I can't help it really. All the other mums (except for Alice's of course) seem to be kinder, and easier, and just more fun. It's not fair. How come I got stuck with the crazy mum? The one who is on a permanent crusade? When all the other mums are fussing about their hair and their clothes, my mum is busy trying to save the world, or the universe. She always thinks she's right, and maybe she is, but I don't care, I just wish she'd chill out and relax a bit.

Anyway, one Friday a few weeks later, she was her usual bossy self, and it seemed that she had found yet another way to make me seem like a total loser. Then, on the Saturday, she did something which was so completely and wonderfully out of character that I thought for a while that I'd died, and been reborn into a normal family.

Anyway, this is what happened. On Friday, when I got home from school, Mum was ranting and raving because there was a piece in the paper saying that someone is planning to build a new housing estate which will take a big chunk out of the park. Her face was all red, she was so cross.

'Can you believe it, Megan? Can you?'

I shrugged. I didn't care much either way. I'm too big for parks.

'They are going to steal our park, our only

green area from us. How can we stand by and let them do this?'

She stopped and I realized that she was waiting for an answer. I made a big mistake.

'Well, you always say the park is full of druggies. You never let me go there. Wouldn't it be better if it was turned into a housing estate?'

Now Mum's face nearly went purple. She actually hit her head with her hand.

'My own daughter! What kind of a child have I raised? How can you suggest that we just concrete over our problems instead of dealing with them properly?'

I spoke in a small voice. 'I was joking, Mum.' I hadn't been joking of course, but I thought that might calm her down. She didn't even hear me though. She ran into the playroom and got one of Rosie's old paintings. On the back she drew a plan of how the park could look if the wild areas were cleared, and if a keeper was employed to maintain it and scare the druggies away. By now she had that fiery glint in her eyes that always makes me very, very nervous indeed. Then she ran to the computer and started printing out petition sheets. I started to feel sick. She was going to wave these around in public, and humiliate me one more time.

I went and stood behind her.

'Mum, you can't. I mean you wouldn't… You wouldn't go out and ask people to sign these? Would you?'

She gave me a scary kind of smile.

'No, darling. I'm not going to go out to ask people to sign these. You are.'

I argued – of course I did. I argued for a long time. But it didn't do me much good. Sometimes Mum just can't be stopped, and it's easier to give in than to argue any more. And so, some time later I found myself standing outside the local shop, clutching a clipboard.

It was the most embarrassing half hour of my entire life. A few mad old ladies came and signed in faint spidery writing. (They thought it was a petition against bin charges, and I didn't bother to explain that they were wrong.) I didn't get many signatures after that, maybe because I spent most of the time with the clipboard under my coat. Just my luck though, when I did have it out, Melissa passed by, and even though I pulled my hat down over my eyes, she still saw me and came over with a big, false show of interest. She grabbed the clipboard from me, and gave her evil, loud laugh when she saw what it was. For a moment, I considered begging her not to tell anyone at school. Then I got sense. She'd just listen to the begging and then tell everybody anyway. You can't appeal to the better nature of someone who doesn't have one. I wished that Alice was there. Alice would have known what to do. But I just stood there with a stupid big red face, saying nothing, In the end, Melissa went away, but I could hear her laughing even after she went around the corner.

I felt like crying. I wanted to go home, but I knew Mum would kill me for having done so badly. She'd probably have insisted on coming back down with me, and started jumping around and shouting, drawing attention to us, making things even worse.

Just then, Sandra, the nice woman who works in the shop, came out. She looked at the clipboard and smiled at me.

'Has your mum asked you to do this?'

I nodded miserably.

'Why don't you leave this with me, and go for a walk for twenty minutes?'

She took the clipboard from me, and went back into the shop. I didn't know what she was at, but by then I didn't care, so I did what she said anyway. I walked ten times around the block, and when I came back, Sandra had collected three pages of signatures. I felt like hugging her, but resisted – just in case Melissa was still hanging around. Things were bad enough without being seen hugging nice shopkeepers in public.

When I got home, Mum was really pleased. She kept going on and on about how good it made her feel that I worked so hard to improve my environment, and that she felt like she was a success as a mother for having raised such a good, environmentally-aware daughter, and how sorry she was for being cross with me earlier. She went on so long that I felt like throwing up. In the end her gushing did dry up, and I escaped to my room. A while later I could hear Mum on the phone in the hall. I figured she was phoning Dad to tell him the wonderful news about his daughter who was going to save the world. I turned up my radio, and drowned out Mum's voice.

Ten minutes later she tapped on the door. For a moment I felt like hiding under the bed, but I knew she'd track me down anyway, so I just sat there, and said 'come in' in as unwelcoming a voice as I could manage.

She came in and sat beside me, and put one

arm around my shoulder. I braced myself for more praise, but she just said, 'Megan, you've been so good that I've decided to treat you. Dad will mind Rosie tomorrow, and you and I are going to have a great day out.'

It was hard to be enthusiastic. Mum's idea of a great day out wasn't likely to be much fun for me. She was probably going to take me to a compost-making workshop or something. Still, it was only polite to ask.

'Where are we going?

She just gave me a huge grin and said.

'Wait and see, Megan. Just you wait and see.'

It almost sounded like a threat.

Chapter six

Next morning, Mum called me at some horribly early hour. It was dark outside, and it felt like it was still the middle of the night.

She tapped me on the shoulder. 'Come on, Megan, get up. We're going on our trip.'

I moaned and turned over. 'Aw, Mum. I'm tired. Can't we go later?' (*Or maybe never.*)

She laughed. 'No, Megan, we can't go later. Now get up and get dressed quickly, if you don't hurry we'll miss the train.'

Suddenly I didn't feel tired any more. I sat up in bed. Mum's 'special trips' usually involved walking, or bikes, or once even a canoe journey. Mention of a train was good news. Maybe we were going to visit my cousins in Mallow. Or maybe she was going to take me to Cork and buy me some vaguely fashionable clothes.

I got dressed as quickly as possible, and ate all my porridge without complaining.

When we were driving to the station, I kept asking, but Mum still wouldn't tell me where we were going, and it was only when we got to the ticket window that I heard the magic words 'An adult and a child day return to Dublin.'

I didn't dare to hope. 'Mum, could I…? I mean….. Are we…?'

She didn't answer. She spent ages putting her change in her purse, and checking that her bag was zipped up safely, and then she turned to me with a big smile. 'Are we what?'

I was so excited I could hardly get the words out. 'Are we going to see Alice?'

She shook her head and the hopes I hadn't dared to hope vanished into the cold, diesel-scented air. Then Mum continued. 'No, *we* aren't going to see Alice. But *you* are. I'm going shopping, and you get to spend the day with Alice.'

I still didn't want to hope. This had to be too good to be true. 'But.... what about her music lessons, and her dad? Isn't she spending the day with him? What if she's not even there? She might be gone out somewhere.'

Mum smiled again. She's really quite pretty when she smiles. She should do it more often. 'Don't worry, love. It's all arranged. I spoke to her mother yesterday. Alice's music lesson will be over by the time we get there, and her dad isn't going up until tomorrow. Now hurry up or we'll miss the train.'

I was so happy that I gave her a huge hug, and

in my mind, I forgave her for the petition thing the day before. I didn't tell her that, though, I didn't want her getting ideas.

The train journey seemed to take forever. Mum proved that she hadn't totally lost it, so instead of tea and chocolate muffins, I got a healthy snack of sunflower seeds and organic apple juice. I didn't care though.

Next we got a taxi to Alice's new apartment. I rang the buzzer, and could hardly stop myself from jumping up and down while I waited for an answer. Then I heard Alice's voice. 'Who is it?' It was funny talking to a metal box. 'It's me. I mean, Megan.'

She laughed. 'Well, come on in. It's the second floor.' There was a clicking noise, and the door opened. Mum kissed me goodbye, and promised to be back to collect me at half past four. I looked at my watch. That was five and a half hours. Heaven. Then I ran up the stairs as fast as if there was a whole crowd of mad park-petitioners after me.

Alice met me halfway up. We both stopped. I felt shy, which was really stupid, since I was only meeting my very best friend in the whole world who I hadn't seen for five long weeks. She looked kind of shy as well, so I didn't feel too bad. Then her mum's voice floated down the stairs. 'Alice O'Rourke, were you by any chance born in a field? Get up here and close that door.'

We both laughed, and all of a sudden everything was OK. Alice put her arm over my shoulder. 'Come on up, Megan. Welcome to my new life.'

When we got into the apartment, Alice's mum came out into the hallway and shook my hand. 'Why, hello Megan. How very nice to see you.' She didn't look like she meant it. As usual she was dressed like a model, all slinky clothes and high-heeled pointy boots.

Then Jamie came over. He looked smaller than I remembered. 'Did you bring sweets?' I shook my head, and he immediately lost interest in me. Alice's mum put on her coat, and bullied Jamie into his. 'Now, Alice. You know I'm trusting you, so you have to be on your best behaviour. I've left you some sandwiches in the fridge. I'll be back at five.'

Then with a click-click of her very high heels she was gone. I could hardly believe it. I grinned at Alice and she grinned at me. Then she took me by the hand and pulled me into her bedroom. She lay on her bed, and I sat on a huge purple beanbag, and we said all the silly things we hadn't been able to say for weeks. She laughed at all my funny stories about Melissa, and she made a face when I told her about the petition the day before.

Then she told me about her school. It sounded just like any other school – pretty boring. Then I noticed that she looked really sad.

'What's wrong, Al? Is it awful?'

She shook her head. 'Not really. The teachers are OK. And some of the girls are quite nice. It's just that I keep wishing that I was back in

Limerick, that's all. I miss Dad. I miss you. Sometimes I think I even miss Melissa.'

I didn't know what to say. Alice was usually so positive, I didn't know how to cope with this new, sad girl.

Then she shook her head like she was trying to push away all the bad thoughts. She jumped up and smiled. 'Anyway, enough moaning. Let's go out for something to eat.'

I was shocked. I'd never been out to eat without an adult before. 'But didn't your mum say she's left us some food?'

Alice laughed. 'Oh, yeah, that. Let's check it out.' She led me back into the kitchen, and pulled open the fridge door. She took out a plate covered in foil. She peeled back the foil and revealed a stack of small white sandwiches with the crusts cut off. She put her nose down and sniffed. 'Yuck! Tuna. I'm not eating these.'

I actually quite like tuna sandwiches, especially when I don't have to eat the crusts, but I didn't like to say so.

She threw them into the bin, and covered them up with an old newspaper. Then she grabbed her coat and led me to the hallway.

'Come on, Megan. It's time for your tour.'

We had a lovely few hours. We went to a fast food restaurant and had a giant bag of chips. Then we bought a monster ice-cream each. Then we hung around a shopping centre, looking at the clothes and the CDs and the jewellery. We bumped into a girl from Alice's class, Janine, and we chatted for a few minutes. She seemed nice and friendly, but I felt so jealous it gave me a pain in my head. I couldn't bear the thought of Alice having a best friend who wasn't me. When she'd gone, I tried to act casual. 'Do you like her?'

Alice thought for a moment. 'Yeah. She's nice.'

It was like a knife twisting in my heart. Then Alice continued. 'But she's not half as nice as you.' I felt a lot better then.

After that, we went for a walk, and got more

chips and then it was four o'clock.

We went back to Alice's apartment. Alice rooted around the kitchen and found some chocolate biscuits. We took them into her room, but I didn't feel like eating them. I felt kind of sick after all the chips. I sat on the beanbag again, and played with the zip of my jacket. I didn't want to go home. I didn't want to leave Alice behind in this place that wasn't home. She was very quiet. She was looking out the window with her shoulders all sort of hunched over. I went over and stood beside her. There was no garden outside – just an ugly old car park. I felt like crying, but that would have been really mean. Alice had much more reason to cry than I had.

She made a sudden kind of a croaky noise. I felt sick. I hadn't seen Alice cry since she was about six. I wondered if I should hug her. Then I looked at her, and saw that she wasn't crying. She was laughing. As I watched, she turned to me and laughed out loud. For a minute I thought that she had gone completely mad. She looked like she had completely lost it.

'What is it, Al? What's so funny?'

'I'll tell you what's so funny, Megan. I've just had the most wonderful idea ever. I have a plan.'

'What kind of plan?'

She laughed again. 'A plan to put an end to all this. A plan so you and I can be together again.'

Now I knew she'd gone mad. Nothing would persuade her mother to move back to Limerick. I felt sorry for Alice again. She'd have to tell me about her plan, and I'd have to be the one to tell her all the reasons it wouldn't work. Sometimes, being the sensible one in a friendship was very hard work.

I sighed. 'So tell me about your plan.'
She shook her head. 'No, I won't. You'll only tell me it won't work.'

I went red, but she didn't seem to notice. She went on talking. 'But it will work, I promise. I just have to work out a few details.'

Now I was interested. 'Please, Al, tell me.'

She shook her head. 'No, Meg. Sorry. Just trust me for once. I'll tell you when I see you again.'

'But when will that be? I know Mum won't bring me up here again.'

She shrugged. 'Well, sometime soon, Mum will have to let me go to Limerick. Don't worry, I'll see you soon, and everything will be fine, I promise. All will be revealed the next time I see you.'

Alice was good at keeping secrets. I knew there was no point in pushing her. And also, I knew that underneath all her laughing and joking, she really was very unhappy. She missed her dad, and she missed her old life. She was my best friend, and it was my duty to help her. I had a funny feeling that however mad or crazy her plan was, I'd end up helping her to put it into action.

Just then, I saw a taxi pulling up outside. Mum got out and walked to the entrance of the apartment building. The buzzer in the hall went.

Alice walked me downstairs. She chatted to Mum for a minute, and then winked at me when Mum wasn't looking. Then Mum checked her watch.

'Sorry, girls, but we have to go. I don't want to miss the train.'

Alice and I had a quick hug, and then I got into the taxi with Mum. I looked back as we drove off. Alice was still grinning madly, and for one precious minute, I really believed that she could fix everything.

Chapter seven

It was strange going back to school on Monday. Everything was just like before, and it was kind of like the weekend had never happened. I wanted to tell someone about my trip to Dublin, but the only person I could think of was Miss O'Herlihy, and telling the teacher was too sad for words. So I didn't tell anyone.

Melissa had sprained her arm on Saturday, and everyone was fussing over her so much that she didn't get a chance to tease me about the petition. Fingers crossed, I thought, with any luck she'll forget about it altogether.

*   *   *

And so a few weeks went by, boring, just like before. As usual, Alice e-mailed me every few days. I wanted to send her a message every day but Mum wouldn't let me. She said that would make me seem desperate. I was desperate of course, but I couldn't tell Mum that. She'd only have started one of those serious talks I hated. And I couldn't sneak a message without Mum knowing because she won't tell me the password for the computer. She thinks the Internet is a dangerous place for kids. When she said that, Dad said the world is a dangerous place anyway and why not just lock me up in an ivory tower altogether and be done with it. Then Mum gave Dad one of her not-in-front-of-the-children looks and that was the end of that.

Alice and I took turns to phone each other on

Saturdays. I never had much to say. Alice always had lots. She was making friends. She mentioned Janine a few times. Even though I was glad for Alice, I couldn't help feeling a bit jealous too. Sometimes she mentioned her secret plan, but I pretended not to be interested, even though I was dying with curiosity.

Then, just before Halloween, I got the e-mail I was waiting for.

Dear Meg,

The best news ever ever ever!!!!!! I'm coming home at Halloween. Jamie can't come because he has a soccer match (yippee!) so it will be just me and Dad. I'll be coming down on the train. And I can see you every day. It'll be fantastic. Mum says I can stay for three days. She said it would be unsettling to stay for longer

than that... I didn't argue too
much, because of THE PLAN. I
can't say any more in case
anyone else reads this. Does
your mum read your messages?
Mine doesn't, but that's only
because she still can't work
the computer. (Let's hope she
never learns.) Anyway, I'll
e-mail you again soon, and I'll
see you in sixteen days. I
can't wait.
Al xxxxxx

Those sixteen days were very long. It felt more
like sixteen hundred days. Every night I crossed
off another day on the calendar over my desk in
my bedroom. Mum said that wouldn't make
them go any faster, and she was right, but I continued anyway. I hadn't anything else to do.

At last it was the Friday of mid-term. I was so
happy, I felt like shouting and screaming and

dancing out of school. (Of course I didn't do it. Melissa and her buddies would never ever let me forget something like that.) Even so, I found myself giving an odd little skip every now and then as I walked home.

When I got home I changed out of my uniform, and hung it in the wardrobe, shoving it right to the back. After all, I wouldn't be wearing it again for ten more wonderful, happy, Melissa-free days. I put on my best jeans and the top Mum bought me on the day Alice had left. Then I sat in my room and waited. I tried to read my new Jacqueline Wilson book, but I couldn't concentrate. I was reading the words and turning the pages, but I had no idea what was happening in the story.

It was a long wait. It was nearly six o'clock before I heard Alice's dad's car stopping outside. I ran out to the front door. Alice was just getting out of the car. I hadn't seen her for five whole weeks. She looked just the same. She had a new denim jacket, and great new jeans.

'Meg!' she shouted, when she saw me, and she ran over to me. We even hugged.

Her dad smiled. 'Oh, hello, Megan. I see you two are glad to see each other. Would you like to come inside with Alice for a while?'

I knew Mum would give out to me later for 'invading their privacy', but I didn't care.

'I'd love to thanks,' I said. Alice put her arm around me and we went inside.

It was funny being in her house again. I'd spent half my life there before, but hadn't been in there since Al had left. It was tidy, but it was very cold. Al's dad went upstairs with her bag, and Al and I went into the family room. All of Al's books were still on the shelf, and Jamie's toys were in the corner where they always used to be. They used to have a fancy black and white family photo-graph hanging over the fireplace, but it was gone.

I sat on the beanbag, and Al lay on the leather

couch. With her shoes on. She noticed me looking at her feet.

'That's one of the good things about being
from a broken home. There's different rules.
Mum would kill me for putting my feet on the
couch, but Dad doesn't care. And in Dublin, I
can leave doors open, and lights on, because
they're the things Dad hates, so Mum just lets me
do them. She doesn't care, as long as I don't mess
the place up, or make too much noise.'

I laughed. Even being in the same room as Al
again made me feel good. There were loads of
things I wanted to tell her, but first there was the
one big thing I had to ask. I took a deep breath.

'Come on, Al. Now's the time. What's your
secret plan? How are you going to get us back
together again?'

She looked towards the door, and whispered.
'I'm not going back to Dublin on Monday.'

I was so delighted that I forgot all about the
plan. 'Hey, that's great. Are you staying for the

whole week? Your dad must be pleased. But how did you get your mum to change her mind?'

Al put on one of the mysterious looks that I knew so well.

'She didn't change her mind. That's the plan. She thinks I'm going back, but I'm not.'

Alice was my best friend, but even I had to admit that she sometimes had crazy ideas. She kind of got all excited, and forgot that she was living in the real world, not a nice, easy, story-book kind of world. She always thought life could be like the movies.

I looked at her. She was lying back on the couch, like she was all relaxed, but her eyes had that wild, crazy kind of sparkle, that always made me a little bit afraid.

I had to ask.

'But won't your dad just make you go back?'
She smiled.

'Well, actually, he won't know anything about it.'
I tried not to sound too suspicious.

'How exactly are you going to fix that?'

She gave me a big grin.

'Easy. You're going to help me.'

I smiled nervously. Nothing was ever as easy as Alice thought it would be. Still though, I didn't really care. It was great to have her back, and if she had a way to stay for longer than three days, I was all for it.

Just then, the doorbell rang. It was Rosie, looking all cute in her dalmatian dressing-gown and pink furry slippers.

'Meggy. Home,' she said, looking very pleased with herself.

I sighed. 'Sorry, Al. I know there's no point arguing with Mum. I have to go. And I know she won't let me back after tea. She'll just say you need "quality time" with your dad. I know she won't let me out again. Will your dad let you call over do you think?'

She grimaced. 'I don't think so. He wants us to have pizza together. And I'm really starting to hate pizza. And he's rented a movie. I saw it ages ago, with Mum, but I can't tell him that, can I? I'll have to see you in the morning.'

Just then her dad appeared in the hall, so I couldn't ask any more about Al's big plan. She was probably very pleased about that. She loved dragging things out, keeping me in suspense.

Her dad had the phone in his hand.

'Sorry for interrupting girls, I'm just going to order the pizza. Pepperoni for you, Alice?'

Alice made a face behind his back, and put her finger in her mouth, pretending to be sick.

'Sounds great,' she said. 'Just what I want.'

I had to run out the door so her dad wouldn't see me laughing. I just gave a little wave, behind my back, and went home to my organic pasta.

Chapter eight

Next morning I woke real early, and I got dressed straightaway. No point though, because of course Mum wouldn't let me go next door. She was afraid Alice and her dad wouldn't be up yet.

She suggested what she thought was a great idea.

'Why don't you do all your jobs now, so later, when Alice is up, you'll be free to play with her?'

(I was twelve years old. Didn't she know that twelve-year-olds don't play? Twelve-year-olds just hang out.)

So I spent an hour hoovering, and dusting, and helping Mum clean out the utility room. Every now and then I had a little grumble.

'No one else has to do as many jobs as I do. Melissa doesn't do a single thing.'

Mum had her usual answer. 'Well, I'm not Melissa's mum, am I? I can't help it if she's allowed to be a spoiled brat. And anyway, since when do you care about Melissa?'

I shrugged. 'I don't. It's just that I seem to do more jobs than anyone I know. It's not fair.'

Mum put on her serious voice then.

'I know love. It doesn't seem fair. But I don't want you thinking that the house tidies itself. It doesn't, you know. I have so much to do, and if you don't help, I'll never get through it.'

I looked at her. She did look a bit tired. So I worked even harder, jumping whenever she asked me to bring something upstairs, or to put something in the bin. By half past nine, the house looked perfect to me.

Mum sighed. 'Now for the hall cupboard.'

I groaned and Mum gave a big laugh.

'Just kidding. The hall cupboard will wait. You go and call for Alice.'

She gave me a hug, and a kiss on the cheek.

'And thanks for all your help.'

I pretended to wipe the kiss away with the sleeve of my fleece, but I was pleased.

Alice opened the door as I approached her doorstep, as if she'd been waiting for me.

'At last. I've been up for hours. Dad wouldn't let me over. He said it was too early.'

'Yeah. Me too. And I've had to do loads of jobs for Mum. You'd think the president was coming to visit.'

'Well, it was worse for me. After breakfast, Dad made me look at old photographs with him. And he got all sad whenever he came to ones of the four of us. His voice kept going all funny, and I thought he was going to cry.'

'Oh no. Gross! What did you do?'

She giggled.

'I gave him a speech I heard on telly last week. I said I wanted to be positive, and look ahead, and all that old stuff. So we played Boggle instead. It was boring, but it was worth it. It's awful you know. Mum and Dad are the grown-ups, but I spend all my time minding them, as if they were the children. I have to be careful all the time. If I'm happy, it's as if I don't care that they've separated. And if I'm sad, they go all guilty on me.'

For the first time, I had kind of an idea what it must be like for her.

'Oh, I'm sorry, Al. Is it awful?'

She nodded. Then she brightened suddenly.

'Come on upstairs. We have to talk.'

We went upstairs to her bedroom. It was really untidy, as usual, with clothes strewn everywhere. Around her bedhead there was a string of pale pink flowery lights. They looked really cool.

Alice saw me looking at them.

'Dad got them for me. He keeps buying me stuff. It's the guilt thing again. I'd prefer if things were back the way they used to be though. I could live without these lights.'

I felt the petals. They were made of a shimmery, pearly kind of plastic, and were really pretty. Like something in a rich kid's house.

'You can borrow them if you like – when I'm not here,' offered Alice.

I sighed.

'Thanks, but no thanks. You know what my mum's like. She'd just say they were a waste of electricity, so she wouldn't let me plug them in. There'd be no point.'

Alice imitated my mum's voice. 'Girls, don't you know anything about global warming? What do they teach you at school these days?'

I giggled. Alice was a very good mimic.

I sat on her new blow-up chair. 'Now. I'm fed

up of waiting. Tell me your plan.'

Alice threw herself onto her bed, and wriggled in excitement. 'It's one of my best. It's a classic. Simple, but effective.'

She looked at me intently. 'Simple is always the best. Then there's less to go wrong.'

I was impatient. 'Cut the waffle, and tell me. What's your plan?'

She smiled. 'Well, you see, I'm going to pretend to go back to Dublin, but I won't. Dad will think I'm with Mum, and Mum will think I'm with Dad. Like I said, it's simple. They'll ....'

I interrupted her. 'Yeah, but if you're not with your mum, and not with your dad, where exactly *will* you be?'

'That's the great part. I'll be staying in your house.'

My heart sank. Here was the big flaw I'd been afraid of. This plan could never work. I decided it was best to tell Alice now, before she got too excited. 'Sounds like fun, but my mum and dad will never agree to let you stay. Not if your parents don't know. You know how parents always stick together. It's like they have some secret code of honour or something.'

Alice laughed. 'That's the best thing of all. That's what makes this plan so brilliant. Your mum won't know I'm there. I'll be in hiding. I'll be like a hostage. I'll sneak into your room, and no one will know, except for us.'

Already I could see all kinds of problems, but then I suppose that was the difference between me and Alice. I always saw problems where she saw opportunities. 'How long do you think we'll get away with this? Until you're eighteen?'

Alice shook her head impatiently. 'Of course not. I'm not a complete dork you know! Dad will go up to Dublin on Friday to visit me, and I won't be there.'

That sounded like real trouble. 'They'll go crazy.'

Alice was unconcerned. 'Well, I suppose they'll panic a bit. That's the whole point.'

'And then?'

'And then, before they get really scared, and before they get time to call the guards, I'll ring and tell them I'm safe, and they'll be all happy and relieved.'

I thought I could see where all this was leading. 'And then they'll get back together, and the four of you can live happily ever after? I'm sorry Al, but I don't think it'll be that easy. I think you've watched *The Parent Trap* once too often.'

Alice shook her head. 'Did I mention the fact that I'm not a complete dork? I know that won't happen. That would never happen. But if Mum finally sees how upset I am about the move, she might just feel sorry enough for me to move back to Limerick. It's not like she's got a job or anything in Dublin. She could easily come back here. She could move into one of the new apartments around the corner, and I could go back and forth between her and Dad whenever I liked. It could be almost as good as before. Maybe even better. I wouldn't have to listen to Mum and Dad fighting all the time. And I could go back to school with you. And we could do stuff after school. It would be the best thing ever.'

She gave me a huge smile, and all of a sudden the whole thing seemed wonderful, and fantastic and not at all impossible.

Chapter nine

Step one of the big plan was to make sure Alice's dad wasn't around on Monday afternoon, when she was supposed to be catching the train back to Dublin. That was easy. We approached him after lunch on Sunday, when he was relaxing in their living room with the papers.

Alice kind of sidled up behind him, and sat on the arm of his chair. She put on her sweetest voice. I thought it sounded a bit over the top, but her dad didn't seem to notice.

'Dad, are you playing golf this weekend?'

He smiled at her. 'No love. I want to spend time

with you, since I see so little of you these days.'

'But Dad, I don't mind, honestly. I know how much you love playing golf. Isn't there a competition on tomorrow afternoon?'

We knew already that there was. We'd checked it in the local paper.

Alice's dad sat up, and began to look interested. 'Well, now you mention it, there is actually. I could…'

He hesitated. 'No, I couldn't. How would I get you to the station?'

Now it was my turn. My voice was even sweeter than Alice's.

'My dad has already offered. He has to pick up some things from his office tomorrow evening. It wouldn't be any trouble. He says it's fine.'

Alice's dad looked closely at me. I opened my eyes wide and tried to look innocent. I'd never be as pretty as Melissa, but luckily I was blessed with the kind of face that adults seemed to trust. I smiled my best smile.

It worked. He looked at Alice again.

'And you're sure you don't mind?'

She smiled at him. 'Quite sure.'

He thought for a moment.

'You know, you're two very considerate girls. I haven't played golf for weeks. It would be good to get out to hit a few balls. I'll just run next door, and thank your dad, Megan.'

He got up and went towards the door.

I had to think fast. 'No, don't. It's fine. He's busy. He's very busy actually. He's em, em.... He's changing Rosie's nappy.'

Alice added. 'She's got terrible diarrhoea. It's not a pretty sight, I promise. And the smell! Think really really gross, and then double it. It's like ...'

I gave Alice a funny look. She was getting carried away as usual. She stopped talking and I continued. 'It just isn't very nice, believe me.'

Her dad sat down again. Luckily he didn't know that Rosie hadn't worn a nappy for at least a year.

'Oh, fine so. I'll thank him the next time I see him. Alice, get me the phone, won't you? I must ring up and book a tee-time.'

Alice got him the phone, and then we ran upstairs. We gave a quiet cheer and a high-five. Success! Step one was done and dusted.

* * *

Next day, I stood in my front garden and watched Alice hugging her dad, as he was leaving for golf.

'See you Friday, love. Only four days. Isn't that nice? Tell your mother I'll be there around seven.'

She beamed at him. 'Yeah Dad. I will. Only four days. Great.'

He gave her one more hug, then he checked his watch, and jumped into the car. He wound down the window, and looked at me.

'You're sure it's OK with your mum and dad? Should I go in and talk to them?'

Alice put on her exasperated voice. 'Dad,

relax. Take a chill-pill or something. I'm spending the afternoon with Megan. I've already
brought my stuff into her house, and her dad will
drive me to the station at five o'clock. It's all
sorted. Now go and play your golf before it's too
late. Love you.'

She leaned in and kissed his cheek, and then he
drove off.

It was a lovely afternoon. We spent a lot of
time playing basketball shots, and chatting, just
like in the old days. It was a nice feeling, knowing
that we were going to be together so much for
the next few days.

At five o'clock, we went into the sunroom of
our house. Dad was dozing, Rosie was playing
with her dolls on the floor, and Mum was reading the paper. '

Alice has come to say goodbye, Mum. She has
to go now.'

Mum looked up from her paper.

'Oh dear. The weekend went so quickly, didn't

it? Long weekends are never quite long enough, are they?' She went to get up. 'I'll wave you off.'

Oh no. How could I get her to stay inside? If she went out she'd see that Alice's dad's car wasn't there, and everything would be ruined. Sudden drastic action was called for. I did a very mean thing. I leaned down and gave Rosie a quick, hard pinch on the shoulder. Her reaction was immediate. She gave a huge howl, and tears began to pour down her puckered-up face. I mentally promised to give her some sweets later to make up for being so mean. Alice took her chance. 'I'll go so. Dad's waiting. Bye everybody.'

Mum was so busy consoling Rosie that all thoughts of following us were gone.

We went out the front door. We stayed outside for about ten minutes, then I went back in. Rosie was happy again, though she did give me a funny kind of look. Dad was still asleep, and Mum was engrossed in the paper.

'I'm going to my room for a while,' I said.

Mum looked up. I put on a sad face, and she gave me a sympathetic smile. 'Oh, OK dear. I'll call you when it's time for tea. It's pancakes.'

I went to my room. Luckily, I slept downstairs, in what used to be the garage. I even had my own little shower room, right next door. It was a perfect set-up for hiding friends, though I'm sure that's not what Mum and Dad had in mind when they allowed me to move down there.

I opened the bedroom window, and gave a low whistle, the special signal we had agreed earlier. Alice appeared from the bushes at the side of the house, carrying her weekend bag, and the sleeping bag we'd borrowed from her house. She climbed in, and we hid her stuff in the wardrobe. Then we sat on the bed and giggled quietly for a while. I was excited and happy and afraid all at once.

Soon Mum came to call me for tea. Luckily, I'd insisted for the past year that she and Dad knock before coming into my room, explaining that at the age of twelve, I needed some privacy. So when Mum tapped on the door, Alice had plenty of time to roll under the bed, out of sight. It worked fine – but then it should have – she'd practised about a hundred times already.

I ate my tea as quickly as possible, and went back to my room. Poor Alice wasn't happy.

'Oh, Meg. Those pancakes smelled so good. Couldn't you even get me a small scrap?'

I shook my head.

'Sorry, Al. No point taking foolish chances. How could I explain if I was caught sneaking pancakes into my room? Mum never allows me to eat in here.'

She sighed. 'Yeah, I suppose you're right.'

I smiled at her. 'Anyway, don't worry, we've got loads of food.'

I went to my wardrobe and pulled out the bag we'd been filling ever since we'd started to plan. Alice looked inside.

'Hmm. Apples or bananas or biscuits or cream crackers. I don't know where to begin.'

Suddenly all the carefully stashed food looked a bit pathetic, and I felt a bit guilty at the thought of the seven yummy, golden, buttery, lemony pancakes I'd just scoffed.

I spoke encouragingly.

'Don't worry, Al. This is just for tonight. We'll get better stuff tomorrow.'

She shrugged, and bit into an apple.

'Doesn't matter, I can be brave. And it'll all be worth it in the end. You'll see.'

Chapter ten

I went into the living room at eight o'clock that evening. Mum looked up from patching Rosie's pyjamas. Surely I lived in the only family in Ireland where the kids were expected to wear patched pyjamas. I couldn't help commenting, even though I knew Mum wouldn't pay much attention to my opinion.

'Mum, we're not poor. Dad has a good job. Can't you just buy Rosie some new pyjamas? They have lovely ones in Dunnes Stores and they cost less than ten euro.'

Mum sighed. 'Megan, how many times do I have to tell you? It's not about the money. It's about the environment. I can't in conscience throw these pyjamas in the bin just because they're a bit worn at the knees.'

Dad looked up and laughed. 'A bit worn? Actually, Sheila, they're transparent.'

Mum gave him a really filthy look, and he stopped laughing. I was sorry I'd started the whole thing. I spoke as brightly as I could.

'Actually, I just came in to say I'm going to bed.'

Mum put down her sewing and felt my fore-head. 'Aren't you well, love? It's not like you to volunteer to go to bed. Especially when you've no school tomorrow.'

I tried to put on a tired smile. 'I'm fine, Mum, really. I'm just wrecked. I mustn't have slept well last night. I might read for a little while.'

Mum still looked puzzled, but she just said,

'OK so, love. Goodnight. Don't forget to brush your teeth. I'll be in in a while to tuck you in.'

I knew there was no point in arguing. I figured that if I was twenty, Mum would still have to tuck me in at night. I'd be coming home from discos at three in the morning, and Mum would be there in her dressing gown and slippers, waiting to tuck me in.

Alice would just have to be ready to hide when she came.

I kissed Dad, and skipped off to my room. So far, so good.

I changed into my pyjamas, and went into the bathroom next to my room, and locked the door. I opened the window, and gave the whistle signal. Then Alice climbed out through my bedroom window, and in the bathroom window. I climbed out of the bathroom window, and hung around in the garden until Alice was finished. It was very cold. I decided that the next night I'd stay in my clothes for that part. Then Alice climbed out of the bathroom window, and I climbed in. I went to the toilet, did my teeth and washed my face and hands. Then I unlocked the bathroom door, and sauntered back down the hallway to my room.

Alice was waiting for me, lying in her sleeping bag on the floor next to my bed. She laughed quietly.

'Whew. That was kind of complicated, wasn't it? We're going to be very good at climbing by Friday. We'll be ready to tackle Mount Everest.'

I laughed too. 'Just be glad I don't sleep upstairs.'

She sighed.

'Yeah, I suppose. Still, are you sure I couldn't chance just running along the hall to the bathroom?'

I shook my head.

'No way. We're not taking any chances. And I'm not risking you bumping into Mum or Dad. I want this to work.'

It was true. Although I'd been a bit doubtful at first, I was sure by then that Alice had devised a brilliant plan. It had to work. It just had to. All I could think of was having Alice back in Limerick for good. As soon as possible. I wanted us to be in the same class again. I wanted us to make our confirmation on the same day. I wanted us to go to the same secondary school, and still be best friends when we were really old – like seventeen or eighteen or something. And if I had to spend a few days climbing in and out of windows to achieve that, well it seemed to me that was a small price to pay.

Alice looked at her watch and panicked suddenly.

'Oh no, it's time to ring Mum. This is the hardest part, I know. What'll we do if she doesn't believe me?'

I tried to sound confident.

'Of course she'll believe you. Why wouldn't she? It'll be fine, I promise.'

I was a bit worried though. Alice was always the chief planner, and if she got scared, I wasn't sure I could keep things going for long.

Alice looked at me doubtfully as she took out her mobile phone. Then, still in her sleeping bag, she wriggled onto my bed like a giant purple and pink snake. She settled herself on one of my pillows, and dialled her mum's number.

I put my ear next to hers so I could hear both sides of the conversation.

'Hi Mum. It's me, Alice.'

'Oh, hello, dear. I was just getting ready to go to the station to pick you up. Is the train on time?'

'Well, actually, I'm not on the train. I'm feeling a bit sick, so Dad said I could stay here in Limerick.'

Her mum sounded rather impatient.

'Sick? What's wrong? Wasn't Daddy minding you properly? Did he let you catch cold? Isn't that just typical!'

Alice spoke in a soothing kind of voice, like the

one my mum uses with Rosie. 'No, Mum. It's not Dad's fault. I have a bit of a tummy bug, that's all, and I couldn't face the train.'

Her mother gave a long sigh.

'OK. Not much we can do now anyway, is there? I suppose there are no more trains tonight. Can you put Daddy on please?'

Alice hesitated. 'Well, actually, I can't right now. He went out.'

Now her mum sounded really cross. 'Out? Out where? How could he leave you on your own when you're sick? What on earth is that foolish man thinking of?'

'Look, Mum, I'm not going to die, you know. I'm not all that sick. Just too sick to travel. And Dad's been minding me really well all weekend, so I insisted that he go out for a while.'

There was another long sigh from the Dublin end of the phone line. 'OK. I'll see you tomorrow then. Ring me and let me know what train you're on.'

This was the hard part. I held my breath while I waited for Alice to reply.

'Well, actually, I might still be too sick to travel then. I think I'll just stay in bed for the day tomorrow. Megan's mum said she'd keep an eye on me while Dad's at work.'

There was a brief silence, and when Alice's mum spoke again, her voice scored very highly on the crossometer. 'Well, isn't that just typical of your dad, landing you in with strangers while he swans off into work? I'm sure Megan's mum has more to do than keeping an eye on you. We'll have to ...'

Alice suddenly grinned at me. 'Oh, Mum, I think I'm going to throw up. Gotta go. I'll call you tomorrow.' She made a gross, burpy sound into the phone, and then clicked it off. Then she tossed the phone carelessly onto the bed.

I looked at her admiringly. 'Wow, you're such a good liar. I wish I was as good as you.'

She gave a smug little smile. 'It's easy. All you

need is lots and lots of practice. Come on, Meg, you try it, tell me a lie.'

I thought for a moment.

'Em…. Oh, I know – Melissa's the nicest girl I ever met.'

Alice gave me a disappointed look. 'No. I'm not convinced. Try a real lie, but one I might actually believe.'

I thought again. 'OK. How about this? Rosie is a secret genius. I'm the only person in the world who knows that she can speak five languages, and play the guitar better than Bono.'

Now Alice looked really disappointed.

'Well of course I know that's a lie. Bono doesn't play guitar, he just prances around in his sunglasses and sings really cool songs.'

I was a bit annoyed. 'Well, you don't know that do you? Maybe he's the best guitarist in the world. Maybe he just plays for his family.'

Alice was getting cross. 'That's stupid. Just face it, you're wrong. He doesn't play guitar.'

I felt like arguing, but then I got sense. After all, who really cared whether Bono could play guitar or not? And besides, if Alice was going to be hiding in my room for the next four nights, it would be easier if we weren't fighting all the time. She looked at me and smiled. I had a funny feeling she was thinking the same as me.

'Sorry, Meg. Forget it. Let's play "Things we hate about Melissa". You go first.'

I grinned. That was my favourite game, and I was very good at it. 'OK. I really, really hate the way she nods all the time when the teacher is speaking, as if she knew everything already.'

'Oh, yeah. Good one. Now my turn. I really, really hate the way when she puts on her coat, she flicks her hair up, and then checks to see if anyone was watching.'

An hour passed very quickly like that, and then Alice picked up her phone again. This time she dialled her dad's number.

He picked up straightaway. 'Hello.'

He sounded kind of lonely, but maybe I was just imagining that.

'Hi, Dad. It's me, Alice.'

'Oh, hello, darling. Are you home already?'

'Yes, Dad. Safe and sound. I had a lovely weekend thanks. How was your golf?'

He sighed.

'Oh, you know. Good, but not good enough.'

I laughed quietly to myself. He always said that. Alice was more sympathetic.

'Oh, I'm sorry.'

They had some cutie, dreadfully boring father-daughter chat for a few minutes, and then he said, 'Put me on to your mother for a minute, won't you?'

Alice was ready for that. 'I can't, Dad, sorry. She's had to go out for a while. I'm minding Jamie.'

Big mistake.

'Oh, OK. Put Jamie on, so.'

Alice was very quick. 'Oh Dad, I'm sorry. He's

just gone off to sleep. I'll kiss him for you, shall
I?'

Alice wouldn't have kissed her brother unless
she was paid an awful lot of money, but luckily
her dad didn't think of that.

'That's sweet, Allie. Kiss his cute little nose for
me, won't you?'

Alice made a face at me.

'Sure, Dad.'

'Thanks, love. Look, I'd better go. So I'll see
you next Friday, OK?'

Alice gave a huge smile.

'Yes, Dad, I'll see you on Friday.' She clicked
off the phone and continued. '....and by then,
my life will be changing. For the better.'

We gave each other another high five, and a
big hug.

Alice beamed. 'Step two executed, and
successful. We're on our way.'

Chapter eleven

I couldn't relax properly that night until Mum had been in for the tucking-in scenario she loved so much. Actually, I usually loved it too – it made me feel all cosy and safe, like when I was a little girl. But this night was different. I just wanted it over and done with so Al and I could relax and settle down for our first night together.

Alice lay on the floor next to my bed, and we conversed in whispers until, finally, there was a light tap on the door. Alice rolled expertly under the bed, taking her sleeping bag with her.

'Come in,' I said, feeling a bit like one of the three little pigs inviting the big bad wolf into his house.

Mum opened the door and came in. She sat on the edge of my bed. A bad sign. This wasn't going to be a quick kiss and a pat on the head. This was going to be serious.

She put her hand lightly on my shoulder. 'Feeling a bit better now?'

'Mmmm.'

'It's hard, Alice being gone, isn't it? You must miss her an awful lot.'

'Mmmmm.' I couldn't think of anything else to say. Whatever would my mum have said if she knew that Alice was lying only a few inches away from her, inhaling the dust from under my bed, and listening to every word Mum said?

Mum kind of rustled her behind, as if she was settling in.

'You know, Megan, something a bit like this

happened me when I was your age.'

I tried not to look bored. Either my mum was a dreadful liar, or everything that ever happened to me seemed to have happened to her at some stage too.

Mum put on her dreamy kind of voice.

'And guess what?'

I spoke in a sing-song voice.

'I bet it all turned out for the best in the end.'

Mum looked a bit hurt, so I had to add, 'I know, Mum. Thanks for trying to help.'

She smiled and patted my shoulder. 'That's OK. You know we can always talk, don't you?'

She got up to go. At the same awful moment, our eyes fell on a red sweatshirt that was neatly folded on the end of my bed. Mum picked it up, and shook it out.

'What's this? Isn't this Alice's?'

I tried to sound casual. 'Oh yes. We swapped. I gave her my....' I racked my brains trying to think of a jumper that wasn't in the ironing basket, or in the dirty washing pile. Mum always knew where everything was, and I didn't want to be caught out. '... my.... I gave her my blue and white striped one. Just for a loan. Until she comes down again. You don't mind, do you?'

Mum shook her head.

'No, darling, I don't mind. Not if it makes you feel better. Goodnight, darling.'

'Night, Mum.'

I thought she'd go then, but she didn't. She came and sat down on the bed again.

'Remember when you were very small?'

I didn't remember much about when I was very small, but sometimes it seemed like Mum remembered every tiny detail. And she loved to talk about it. At length.

She continued.

'Remember how you used to make me check under your bed every night, in case there was a monster under there?'

Oh no! Why had she suddenly brought that

up? Surely she didn't suspect something? And Mum was big on nostalgia. Was she suddenly going to try to relive old times by checking under the bed? Was this the end of everything?

I put on the most bored voice I could manage. 'That was really stupid, wasn't it?'

She smiled. 'Well, it wasn't so stupid back then. But you're a big girl now, aren't you?'

I smiled back.

'Yes, Mum. Much too big for monsters under the bed.'

She patted my shoulder.

'You're sure you don't want me to check? Just in case?'

I nodded. 'Yes, Mum. I'm quite sure.'

She sat there for a moment longer, and then to my huge relief, she stood up and walked towards the door.

I turned over, and snuggled down under the covers. Mum switched off the light and went out.

After a few seconds, Alice rolled out from under

the bed. She put on a spooky voice. '*I am your worst nightmare. I am the monster from under your bed.*'

I giggled. In the dim light, I could see that she was holding a pair of my dirty socks. 'Yuck, Meg,' she said. 'These stink. How long have they been under the bed?'

I pretended to think.

'Em ... Let me see. Oh yes, they're my communion socks. That'll be nearly four years, then.'

Alice gave a quiet little squeal. I heard the socks hitting the wall over my bed.

'Double yuck. My mum would ground me if I left my dirty washing under my bed. Still though, your mum's nice. She sounded like she really felt sorry for you.'

I sighed. 'Yeah, I know. As mums go, I suppose she's not the worst. She can be a lot of fun. And sometimes she lets us do really crazy things. Do you remember the time she let us make popcorn without putting a lid on the saucepan?'

Alice laughed. 'Oh yeah. Wasn't that mad?'

I got a sudden fit of the giggles. 'Remember how the popcorn flew everywhere, and we raced around, grabbing it, and screaming all the time?'

Alice suddenly stopped laughing. 'Yeah. Fat chance of my mum doing that. If one scrap of food touches the floor she panics, as if it was a major health alert. Your mum's great. You're lucky.'

'Mmmm ... ' I said.

Alice laughed. 'Remember the time, during the World Cup, when your mum used food colouring, and served up green, white and orange mashed potatoes for your dinner?'

I gave a wry smile.

'Hello? Did you just mention my mum, and food colouring in the same sentence? I think not.'

'But I remember it really well. She had the potatoes arranged on the plate in a perfect rectangle, and she had a stick of liquorice or something as a flag-pole.'

This time I had to laugh. 'Oh, yes, I remember all right. But Mum would sooner die than use food colouring. She probably used spinach for the green, and carrot or tomato or something to make the potatoes orange. And if I remember correctly, the flag-pole was made out of a stick of celery. It was all probably a trick to get me to eat even more vegetables.'

Alice didn't care about the details.

'Whatever. All I know is she went to loads of trouble to make dinner fun for you and Rosie.'

Suddenly I started to feel guilty for having a nicer mum than Alice. I tried to think of something not so nice about my mum. It didn't take long. I knew I was being disloyal to my mum, but it was all in a good cause.

'Hey, she's not exactly perfect, my mum. She dresses like she's trapped in the seventies. Sometimes I'm sure she thinks she's the mum in the *Alfie and Annie Rose* books.'

Alice gave a small giggle.

'Hey, now that you mention it...'

I laughed too. 'She has exactly the same hairstyle, and she's been wearing the same roundy glasses ever since I can remember. She always looks like she's just going out to dig the garden. Your mum dresses so nicely. She always looks lovely.'

Alice sighed. 'Yeah, you're right. But she's lovely in an untouchable kind of way. Jamie showed her a painting he did last week, and she kind of backed away from him, making these horrible, panicky squeals in case he'd get paint on her new white jacket. And the other day when I felt really sad about Dad, she kept going on about how she broke one of her new nails. That's not how a mum should behave. She should understand how I feel. That's her job.'

Oh dear. This wasn't working out like I planned. I decided to try again.

'Still though, whenever my mum starts to try to be all buddy-buddy, I feel really, really, embarrassed, and can't wait for her to stop. At her age she should understand the difference between being a mum and being a friend, and concentrate on the things she's good at, like turning our dinner into the Ireland flag. Don't you think so?'

Alice's voice was very quiet, and kind of sad.

'Yes, you're right. But what do you do if your mum's only good at non-mum kinds of things, like bridge, and golf, and putting on make-up?'

She gave a small sob.

'I don't think my mum even likes being a mum. Sometimes I think she's sorry she had me and Jamie. I feel like we're kind of in the way. Like we're spoiling her life.'

I didn't know what to say. Alice had never spoken like that about her mum before. She looked tearful. I leaned over and rubbed her arm. It probably didn't help very much. Alice wiped her eyes, and suddenly she spoke brightly.

'Still. We have to make our plan work. I have to get Mum back to Limerick, and then we'll all live happily ever after. Or something like that.'

I spoke fiercely.

'Our plan will work. It has to.'

Alice nodded and smiled back at me.

After that we talked about Melissa again. We talked about how vain she was, and the irritating way she was always flicking her hair, and generally swanning around the school as if she owned the place. As usual, saying bad things about her and telling each other how much she got on our nerves made us feel much better.

Then we fell asleep.

Day one was over.

Chapter twelve

Day two.

I felt kind of strange when I woke up. A bit sad. A bit happy. A bit excited. And quite a bit afraid.

Alice and I chatted quietly for a while, and then we got dressed. After that we went through the climbing in and out of the window stuff, so Alice could go to the toilet. She laughed when she got back.

'Whew, that was fun. Maybe we could invent a

new sport. We could call it "bathroom mountaineering". What do you think?'

I laughed too. 'Yeah. Sounds great. We could
make videos and everything. We could be rich.'

'And we could be the first world champions.
We could represent Ireland in the Olympics.
We…'

Just then there was a shout from the hallway.
'Megan Sheehan, are you getting up at all today?
And do you want any breakfast?'

Alice scrambled under the bed, dragging her
sleeping bag after her. I called out,

'Yeah, Mum. I'm on my way.'

Then I heard her going back into the kitchen.
Alice rolled out from under the bed, with a big
grin on her face. She loved danger, and I knew
she was really having fun. I often wished I could
be as daring as she was.

I knew Mum would be back if I didn't appear,
so after a few minutes, I wandered into the
kitchen. Rosie was sitting up at the table in her

patched pyjamas, eating a huge bowl of organic porridge. Poor child. She was too young to understand just how sad her life was.

Since it wasn't a school day, I was allowed to have Weetabix – supposedly a big treat. I finished my breakfast, and then I helped Mum to tidy up for a few minutes. Soon Mum went out to the utility room with some empty milk cartons for the recycling bag. Luckily, Rosie toddled after her. As soon as they were gone, I threw two Weetabix into a bowl, grabbed a spoon, and ran to my room with them.

'It's OK, it's only me.'

Alice rolled out from under the bed, and looked at the bowl I was holding towards her. She didn't seem very impressed.

'Don't worry,' I said. 'I'll get milk too. I just couldn't do it all together.'

I wandered back into the kitchen, went to the fridge and poured myself a big mug of milk.

Mum was scrubbing the porridge stains from

the hob, muttering away as she did so. 'What is your dad like? At the age of thirty nine, you'd think that maybe just once he'd be able to cook porridge without letting it boil over. So much for learning through experience.'

I laughed politely, and then said,

'I'm going to read in my room for a while.'

She looked up.

'OK. Are you bringing that milk with you?'

I tried to sound casual. 'Yeah. We were doing nutrition in school last week, and Miss O'Her-lihy told us all about osteoporosis. It sounds awful. I don't want to get that, so I'm going to drink two mugs of milk every day.'

Mum smiled. 'Well, I'm glad she's teaching you something useful. You know broccoli has lots of calcium too?'

I made a face.

'Yeah Mum, but that's going a bit too far, don't you think?'

She laughed, and I escaped with the milk.

Alice finished the Weetabix in double-quick time. She wiped her mouth with the back of her hand. 'Yum. I was so hungry, that was delicious. But I don't think I can survive for the rest of the day on apples and biscuits.'

I sighed. That was going to be a bit of a problem. I'd read loads of stories where kids hide puppies and hamsters in their bedrooms, and struggle to sneak crumbs and rasher rinds to them. I was discovering that sneaking food to a healthy twelve-year-old with a huge appetite was a bit more difficult. Already I was running out of ideas, and besides, Alice was never going to be happy with scraps.

I tried to sound positive.

'Well, don't worry. We can go out for a while this afternoon, and then we can buy you some nice stuff to eat.'

Alice sounded surprised. 'Out? How will we manage that without being caught?'

I smiled and spoke airily.

'Oh, don't worry. I have a plan.'

I felt very pleased with myself. I was getting good at all this secret stuff. Maybe I'd give up on my plans to become a vet and train to be a private investigator instead.

*   *   *

Al and I spent the next few hours in my room. I told Mum I was doing a big clear-out, so she wouldn't be too suspicious. I even tidied a few bookshelves, just in case she came in to check. Then Al and I sat on the floor and chatted and laughed as quietly as we could. After a while we ate some of her biscuit stash. Then, at about twelve o'clock, there was a small rattle, and when I looked around, I could see the handle of my bedroom door turning slowly. Alice was standing by the window, and had no chance to hide. I held my breath as the door opened very slowly, and ... Rosie toddled in. She beamed and held out her arms.

'Alith,' she lisped, as Alice and I stood still in

panic. How could one small three-year-old spoil our great plan? It just wasn't fair.

Then I had a brainwave. I shut the bedroom door, grabbed Rosie and pulled her towards my wardrobe.

'Look, Rosie, sweeties. Lots of nice sweeties for Rosie,' I said, as I rummaged frantically for the secret bag of marshmallows I'd hidden there the week before.

Rosie loves marshmallows, so she was completely distracted for the few seconds it took Alice to roll under the bed. When Rosie's mouth was full, she turned around again. Her mouth opened in surprise, and two marshmallows popped out onto the floor.

'Alith? Alith gone?' she lisped.

I bent down and put my face near to hers, like I'd seen Mum do when she had something important to say.

'Rosie, No Alice. No Alice here. Just me and you. OK?'

She looked a bit puzzled, but happily accepted another marshmallow, and toddled off to look for Mum. I closed the door behind her, and collapsed on to the bed. Then Alice rolled out from underneath and grinned up at me.

At lunch-time, I had another moment of panic when out of the blue Rosie said, nice and clearly:

'Alith gone.'

Mum looked at her, surprised.

'Aaah. Even Rosie misses Alice. Isn't that so sweet? Yes dear, Alice has gone. But I'm sure we'll see her in a few weeks, won't we?'

I was really, really glad that Rosie was only three, and far too young to say something awful like,

'But she was in Megan's room this morning.'

As we tidied up the lunch things, I hid a few slices of bread in the pocket of my hoodie. Not very exciting food, I had to admit, but it was the best I could do under the circumstances. I could hardly bring Alice bowls of soup, or dishes of pasta, could I?

Just as I was leaving the kitchen, Mum turned to me and said,

'I've an idea, Megan. Why don't I leave Rosie with Kathleen up the road for a while, and you and I can have a nice girlie afternoon? Maybe we could go to town. We could go for hot chocolates, and than shop for some new school shoes for you. Wouldn't that be nice?'

Normally, I'd have loved that. But I could hardly skip off to town leaving Alice on her own in my room, could I? It was time for one of my special, reserve ideas. I'd joined the local tennis club a few months earlier, and whenever Mum and Dad couldn't think of anything else to complain about, they'd go on about what a waste of money it had been, since I hardly ever played. It wasn't my fault though. All the other girls who hung out there had been having private coaching since they were about six months old. They were probably playing tennis while they were still in nappies. Once, before I knew any better, Mum persuaded me to enter a competition. I can remember her encouraging smile.

'It'll be an experience, Megan, if nothing else.'

She was right. It *was* an experience. It was the most embarrassing, humiliating experience of my entire life. My opponent, Ciara, had travelled all the way from Cork for the game. Her mother and father had come with her to encourage her. (My parents hadn't thought to travel the half a mile from our house to support me. Which was just as well – I didn't need two more witnesses to my total humiliation.) Ciara had two tennis racquets, like someone who was planning to play in Wimbledon. She was dressed in designer gear from her cute white headband, down to her mega-expensive runners. And she never called when a ball went out – she just did this cool flicking thing with her fingers. After a while, when she realised just how bad I was, she started to apologise every time she sent the ball whizzing past my ear. As if apologising made it better. I only scored two points in the entire match, and that was when she double-faulted. The first time that happened, she threw her racquet on the ground in temper. If my parents saw me do that, they'd have dragged me off the court and grounded me for about six months. Ciara's mother just cooed softly to her:

'Now Ciara, don't forget about your anger management. Breathe deeply and let the tension flow away.'

Sad thing was, Ciara didn't even look embarrassed.

I was put into the competition for first-time losers, but I pretended to be sick, and went home. Mum and Dad met me in the hallway.

'Well, are you our little champion?' asked Dad.

'Do we need to book tickets for Wimbledon?' asked Mum.

I shook my head, and smiled as brightly as I could. 'Oh, it was a good match, but she just about got the better of me in the end.'

I think they knew I was lying, because they didn't ask me any more.

Anyway, after that, who could blame me for being less than enthusiastic about tennis?

Still, Mum was pleased, that afternoon, when I said,

'Thanks, Mum. I'd love to spend the afternoon with you, but I was thinking of going over to the tennis club for a while. Some of the girls in my class said they might be there.'

I felt a bit mean when I saw how happy that statement made her. She gave me a big smile.

'That's great, Megan. I'm glad you're getting on with the other girls in your class. Would you like me to drop you over to the club?'

I smiled back.

'No, Mum. It's fine thanks. The walk will warm me up for the game.'

I ran to my room to change into my tracksuit and runners, and to tell Alice to get ready. A few minutes later, she climbed out the window, and I locked it behind her. Then I got my racquet from the hall cupboard, and called out,

'Bye, Mum. I'll be back in time for tea.'

She came to the door to see me off.

'Bye, darling. Have a good time.'

Luckily I'd told Alice to go out through the gate at the bottom of our back garden. I skipped down the road, and met her at the pre-arranged spot, at the end of the lane.

She stretched her arms high in the air.

'Mmmmm. It's so nice to be out. I'm beginning to feel like a prisoner. Do you think I'll be able to get a loan of a racquet at the club?'

I laughed.

'We are so not going to the tennis club!'

'Why?'

'Too many Melissas there.' (Melissa was our code word for any girl we didn't like.)

Alice looked mystified.

'Where then? Where are we going?'

I smiled.

'Into town.'

Alice was delighted.

'Hey. That's a great idea.'

I was pleased with her reaction. So pleased that I nearly forgot how much trouble I'd be in if Mum discovered I was in town without her knowing. She always said town was full of 'undesirables'. Still, sneaking Alice around was serious enough. If I was caught I was going to be in trouble anyway, and grounded for about a hundred years. I might as well have some fun and make it worth my while.

We ran to the bus stop, and arrived just as a bus pulled up. I felt very grown up indeed, as I bought two tickets, and we set off on our journey.

Chapter thirteen

We had a great afternoon in town. Somehow, everything seems much more fun when you know you're breaking every rule your parents could ever think of. (Plus lots more they haven't got around to thinking of yet.)

First stop was to get Alice a burger and chips. I wasn't hungry of course, since I'd just had lunch, but Alice acted as if she hadn't seen food for days. She stuffed her face, and then very rudely spoke through a mouthful of chips.

'Mmmm. This is so totally yum. I'd forgotten how good warm food could taste.'

I laughed.

'Well, don't get too used to it, we mightn't be able to get out again in a hurry.'

I had the biggest cup of Coke available. (Mum and Dad never allowed me to have Coke, so it tasted extra-nice.)

When Al had finished eating, and I had drained my giant Coke, we wandered out onto the street. I had an idea.

'Let's go into the supermarket. Maybe we can find something for you to eat later.' (I was feeling a bit guilty, because I knew we were having shepherd's pie for dinner, and I couldn't think of a way to smuggle some of that in to Alice.)

In the supermarket, we quickly found the shelf where all the instant-type foods were. I'd never been there before. My mum has a big thing about wholefoods, and fresh fruit and vegetables and organic stuff. Once I heard her saying to Dad that feeding ready-meals to children should be recognised as a form of child cruelty. I picked up a pot of instant noodles, and put on my mum's voice.

'Eugh! Look at this. Full of e-numbers, and hydrogenated fats. Is this food? Or is it a chemistry experiment? How *are* they allowed to get away with this?'

Alice took the pot from me and shook it. She too imitated my mum's voice. (So well that I felt a bit guilty.)

'I think it's just died. And look at this carton. How long will it take for this to decompose?'

I was glum for a moment.

'About as long as it will take my parents to forgive me, if they find out I'm in town this afternoon.'

Alice shook my arm gently.

'Don't worry, Meg, they'll never know. And anyway, we've discussed this. When my parents find me on Friday, I'm taking all the blame. I'll say everything was my fault. It was all my idea.'

I wasn't sure.

'Yes, I know you said that, but I still don't think it's fair.'

Alice spoke firmly.

'Of course it's fair. Remember, I'm the child from the broken home, not you. They'll have to make allowances for my bad behaviour. I'm just acting out my trauma.'

We selected six pots of noodly things that could be heated by pouring boiling water over them, and I tried not to worry too much about how exactly I was going to get boiling water from the kitchen into my bedroom.

After that we did a tour of Cruise's Street. In every shop that sold nail varnish, we each painted one fingernail. It took us about half an hour to get all of them done. We were slowed

down quite a bit by the fact that security guards
chased us out of three shops. You'd think we were
'undesirables'.

Of course, even I knew there was nothing terribly cheeky or bad about trying on nail varnish
in shops, but without Alice, I wouldn't have
dared. That was the great thing about Alice.
When I was with her, I became a better person. I
was braver. And funnier. And happier. Life was
so much more fun when she was around.

We looked at CDs for a while, then jewellery
and clothes. The afternoon went much too
quickly. We got the bus home at half four,
because I knew it would soon be dark. I also
knew that if I wasn't home by dark, Mum would
go to the tennis club to look for me. And if I
wasn't there, she would go into totally, abso-
lutely, crazy panic-mode. She wouldn't stop to
think anything sensible, she'd just presume that
I'd been kidnapped or murdered or something.

Once, in a shop, Rosie slipped out of sight for

a moment and Mum nearly lost her reason. She screeched on the top of her voice.

'Rosie! Rosie! Oh my baby, what's happened to you?'

Two shop assistants came running, thinking someone was dead. Then Rosie appeared from behind a rack of dresses. Mum picked her up and smothered her with big, wet, slobbery kisses.

'Oh, baby, baby. Where were you?'

I thought I'd die of embarrassment, and even Rosie who should have been too young for that looked a little bit uneasy. Then, as if it wasn't quite bad enough, Melissa, with her uncanny knack for being around during my most embarrassing moments, appeared with one of her meanest buddies. They both laughed out loud, and then Melissa whispered to her friend. The only words I could hear were '...*mad mother...*' I felt like shouting at her. '*I know she's mad. But it's not my fault. Why blame me? Do you think I picked her out of a catalogue?*' But of course I didn't. I just

put my head in the air and pretended not to care.
(Even though of course I did. Very much.)

*   *   *

When we got home, Alice took the bag with the
things we'd bought, and sneaked around the
back of the house to wait for me to open my bedroom window. I let myself in the back door, and
ruffled my hair a bit to make it look like I'd been
running around the tennis court. Mum was in
the kitchen as usual. She seemed to live there –
like some kind of enchanted princess, con-
demned to a life of endless drudgery. She was
straining some potatoes.

'Oh, Megan, you're back. It will be dark soon,
and I was just starting to wonder about you. Did
you have a nice time?'

I nodded.

'Yes, it was fine. I might go again tomorrow.'

Mum looked up this time, and smiled at me.

'Well, that is good news. Now will you please
mash these potatoes for me?'

I thought of poor Alice standing in the garden in the cold, waiting for me to let her in my bedroom window.

'OK, Mum, but I'll just run out and put my racquet in the hall cupboard.'

Mum took the racquet from me before I could protest.

'It's OK, I must go check on Rosie anyway. I'll put your racquet away for you. And when you're finished the potatoes, will you empty the dishwasher, and set the table please? Dad will be home soon.'

I didn't want to arouse her suspicions by arguing. It must have been twenty minutes before I got to my room. I opened the window, and gave the signal whistle. There was no reply. I whistled again. All I could hear in reply was the rustling of the trees at the end of the garden. Then I whispered as loudly as I dared.

'Al, Al. Where are you?'

Still nothing. This was awful. Where could she

have gone to?

I climbed out of the window, and ran to the bushes where Alice was supposed to wait for my whistle. She wasn't there. I suddenly began to feel a sense of panic. Where could she be? I ran around the garden, whispering her name as loudly as I dared. At last I found her sitting in Rosie's little old playhouse, right at the end of the garden. She was in a bit of a sulk, but I was so glad to see her, I didn't mind.

She spoke crossly.

'Where were you all this time? I'm frozen.'

'Sorry. Mum gave me loads of jobs. I couldn't get out of the kitchen.'

'You could have said you needed to go to the toilet, couldn't you?'

Suddenly I felt very stupid. Why hadn't I thought of that? Had I no imagination? 'Sorry, Al. I'll say that the next time.'

She brightened suddenly. 'It's OK. Now let's go in, while I can still move my fingers and toes.'

Luckily, I was first to climb in the bedroom window. I was sitting on the window-sill ready to jump down, when I realised that Mum was on her hands and knees, looking under my bed. I had just time to be grateful that we'd hidden Alice's sleeping bag and clothes in the back of my wardrobe, when Mum looked up in surprise.

'Megan! What on earth are you doing there? Were you out in the garden?'

I nodded.

'Er, yes.'

'But it's dark outside. What took you out there at this time of the evening? And why on earth are you climbing in through the window?'

I thought as quickly as my panicked brain would allow. Alice was much better at instant lies than me, but I could hardly shout out to her for ideas, could I? She was only a metre away, but I was very much on my own. I did my best.

'Em …I …you see…I ….. well, actually I….what happened was…..' Even in my panic I knew I was being totally pathetic.

For once in her life Mum didn't want a big long discussion. She stood up.

'Well, whatever. I must finish off the dinner before Dad gets here. Just get down and shut the window, and don't be so silly again.'

I jumped down and closed the window, smiling out into the darkness, just in case Alice was watching. Suddenly I was a bit worried. What had Mum been doing? Did she suddenly suspect something strange? She didn't normally look under my bed. I had to ask.

'Er, Mum, why were you looking under my bed?'

She sighed.

'I think Rosie's hidden the television remote control again. Every time I ask for it, she just laughs. She's being a right little monkey. And your dad will go crazy if it's not there when he wants to watch TV tonight.'

I gave a small sigh of relief.

'Oh, is that all? I'll help you look for it later, will I?'

Mum smiled.

'Thanks, love.'

Then she went out and closed the door, and when I was sure she wasn't coming back, I opened the window once more and let Alice in. She sat down on my bed and she didn't look terribly happy.

It was turning into a very long day.

Chapter fourteen

Dinner that evening seemed to take forever. Mum told Dad about me spending the day in the tennis club, and the two of them went on and on about it, like I'd just been awarded the Nobel Prize or something. They kept saying totally stupid things like:

'Isn't it lovely to see Megan getting some independence?'

And:

'Physical activity is so important. And tennis is *such* a lovely game.'

And:

'It's such a sociable sport. If you play tennis you'll never be without a friend.'

I was sure that if I didn't get back to my bed-room quick, I'd be without Alice as a friend, she'd be so cross and fed-up. In the end, Rosie rescued me by throwing up all over the dinner table. It was totally gross, but at least it distracted Mum and Dad for a while, so I could concentrate on thinking of a way to get boiling water in to my bedroom for Alice's noodles.

Much, much later, when I got back to my room, I still hadn't any good ideas.

'It's not my fault, Al!' I protested. 'Mum never seems to leave the kitchen. She always says she's chained to the kitchen sink, and I'm beginning to think she might be right.'

Alice wasn't sympathetic. 'Well, we'd better think of something. I'm starving.'

She picked up a pot of noodles and shook them. They made a nice rattly kind of sound. I wondered if Miss O'Herlihy would let me play them in the school band.

Alice sighed. 'This is torture. I could die of hunger here, in this very room.'

Things were getting desperate. I'd been best friends with Alice for nearly eight years, and I knew all there was to know about her. And one of the things I knew very well was that when Alice was tired or hungry, she wasn't much fun to be with.

'I know,' I said brightly. 'Mum has the hot water on for Rosie's bath. Maybe if I fill your pot from the hot tap in the bathroom, it would work.'

Alice looked a bit doubtful.

'I'm not so sure. But we'd better try something. I haven't got long left.' As she spoke she sucked her cheeks and her tummy in, and flopped onto the bed in a mock faint.

'Very funny. You just lie there being totally dramatic, and I'll do all the work,' I muttered as I stuffed a pot of noodles into the pocket of my hoodie, and went into the bathroom. I ran the hot tap for ages, but it never got that hot. Not considering I needed water that was actually boiling. In the end I got fed up, and I ripped the foil from the top of the carton anyway. Inside was really gross looking. Maybe Mum was right, it couldn't have been good for you. It didn't even look like food. It was a strange orangey colour, and was mostly dust with a layer of strange-looking brown things on top. I carefully filled the carton up to the mark on the side, and stirred it with the handle of my toothbrush. It actually smelt quite nice – a bit like pizza. I checked to see that the coast was clear, then I ran back to my room. Alice was lying on the bed, trying to look weak.

'Oh, at last. You might have to feed me. I have no strength left.'

'Here,' I said. 'Feed yourself. I worked hard for this.'

Alice took out the spoon we'd saved since breakfast, and dipped it into the pot. She stirred around, and sniffed for a while. 'Mmmm. Smells nice enough. A bit like pizza.'

I smiled to myself. 'Try some then. Before it gets cold.' What I really meant, of course, was 'before it gets colder,' since it was only barely warm to start with.

She gingerly scooped up some of the orange-brown stuff, and put it into her mouth. I smiled at her encouragingly. Behind my back I had all my fingers crossed.

'Yeeurgh.' She very rudely spat it back into its pot. 'Yuck! The noodles are still rock hard. I can't eat this. It's like eating gravel.'

I was upset. 'Come on, Al. Please try. You have to eat. It can't be all that bad.'

She thrust the pot towards my face. 'OK, You try it then.'

I shook my head. 'Sorry, I'm quite full.'

'Yeah. Full after your dinner. Was it nice? Did you have second helpings?'

All of a sudden Alice began to cry. She put her head in her hands, but I could see tears squeezing between her fingertips.

I picked up the pot and put it on my dressing table. I really didn't need to have that stuff spilled on my duvet. It looked like the kind of stuff that would make a stain that would never come out – even with the kind of biological washing powders my Mum refuses to use. 'Oh, Al. I'm sorry. Don't worry. I'll get you some food. I'll think of something, I promise. You won't starve.'

She looked at me crossly, wiping away her tears. 'I know I won't starve. But I'm not just crying about the food. It's everything. I don't think this plan is going to work. We're just going to be in terrible trouble, and then I'll have to go back to Dublin, and it will be worse than ever. Mum won't even let me visit here any more after this. Oh, Meg, this was all a huge mistake.' She put her head down again and gave a succession of huge, sad sobs.

There was no way I was giving up though. No way. There was too much at stake.

I took her by the shoulders. 'Come on, Al. Don't talk like that. Just wait till Mum brings Rosie upstairs for bed, and I'll get some boiling water. You can have two pots of noodles, or three if you want, and you'll feel better, and then we'll plan for tomorrow. We're going to make this work. You just wait and see.'

She looked at me closely. 'Promise?'

I nodded, feeling a bit guilty because the truth of the matter was that I was no longer very sure of anything.

*   *   *

Later, when Mum took Rosie up for her bath, I persuaded Dad to go into the garage to look for some tennis balls for me, and I managed to get a huge jug of boiling water into my room. Alice ate three pots of noodles, and afterwards she was in much better form.

At about eight o'clock, it was time to phone Alice's mother. She answered at once.

'Alice, is that you? Where are you? I've been

phoning the house for ages.'

Whew, I thought, that was lucky. Her dad must have gone out.

Alice spoke airily. 'Oh, I'm home now. Dad took me to the doctor's.'

Her mother sounded anxious. 'Doctor's? Are you that sick?'

'No, Mum. The doctor says I'm fine. It's just a bug. He says I'd better not travel for a few days yet.' She hesitated. 'Maybe I should wait until Friday, and travel up with Dad?'

She had no intention of doing that of course. The whole point was that her Dad would arrive in Dublin without her, and there would be a big panic, and her mother would be shocked into moving back to Limerick.

Her mum spoke. 'Hmmm. I don't know. It's Tuesday now, isn't it? I'll have to see. I need to speak to your father, put me on to him.'

'Well, actually, he had to go back into work. He left early you see, to bring me to the doctor, so he had to go back in again. I think he's going to be home very late.'

Her mother sounded cross again. 'Typical. And of course the switchboard at work won't be on, will it?'

Alice grinned at me. 'No, Mum. Unfortunately not.'

Her mum made a cross, grunting kind of noise. 'And I don't suppose he's entered the twenty-first century and bought himself a mobile phone since I saw him last, has he?'

Alice grinned at me again. 'No, Mum. Sorry.'

'You know what, Alice? I think he deliberately stays out of reach.'

I think she was right. If I was married to a cross woman like her, I'd want to be out of reach occasionally too.

Alice spoke softly, like to a child. 'Don't worry, Mum. It's fine. Why don't I just tell Dad I'll stay here until Friday? He can drive me to Dublin after work and we'll see you then. Isn't that the best thing?'

Her mother gave a big, long sigh. 'Well, we'll see. Don't eat anything until you're better, and tell Dad to get you some Seven-Up to drink, and I'll ring you tomorrow.'

'OK, Mum. I'll phone you though. I've loads of credit on my mobile, and I might as well use it up.'

'OK, bye darling.'

'Bye Mum. Love you.'

Alice clicked off the phone, and grinned at me. I felt a lot better. With every passing day, and with every phone call, it seemed as if we were getting closer to our goal. If only things kept going like this, everything would be perfect. Soon Alice would be back living in Limerick where she belonged, and before long the dried noodles and the bathroom mountaineering would only be a distant memory.

Chapter fifteen

Later that night, when I was pretending to be all settled down in bed, Mum came in to say her goodnights. She still had her apron on, which meant she was busy, so I was confident it was going to be a short session.

As usual, I was wrong.

She sat on the bed and sniffed the air. 'What's that smell?'

I shrugged and tried to look innocent – a look I was beginning to perfect.

'What smell? I don't get a smell.'

I wondered was it Alice's feet. She hadn't dared to have a shower since she'd arrived in our house. And sometimes her feet did pong a bit – especially when she wore trainers.

Mum looked puzzled. 'There's definitely an unusual smell in here. It's like ...'

'Maybe it's that nice perfume you and Dad gave me for my birthday. I put some on earlier.' This wasn't actually a lie. I held my wrist towards Mum's face so she could smell it.

'No, love. It's not that. It's ...'

'Or it could be nail varnish remover, or deodorant or something,' I offered helpfully.

Mum shook her head, and wrinkled up her forehead. 'No. It's nothing like that. I was going to say it's something like onions, or tomatoes or something. Only kind of artificial. Like packet soup.'

Of course. It wasn't Alice's feet that were the

problem. Mum was smelling the stupid pot noodles. She wasn't far off the mark with her guesses. I bet she was a bloodhound in her last life.

I couldn't think of anything to say. All I could think of were the empty noodle pots which were in a plastic bag in a drawer next to my bed.

She shook her head. 'Anyway, whatever that smell is, it's not very pleasant. Will I open the window and let some fresh air in?'

To open the window, she'd have had to go around to the other side of my bed, and even though Alice had rolled underneath, I didn't want to take any chances.

'No, Mum, it's fine thanks. I don't notice anything.'

She sat on the bed, and rubbed my forehead.

'Are you OK, Megan? You look a bit pale.'

I put on a brave smile. 'I'm fine. I'm a bit tired, that's all.'

For once, I wasn't lying. All the fussing over hiding and feeding Alice, and the regular bouts of bathroom mountaineering, were beginning to wear me out. I wasn't used to such an exciting life.

Mum didn't know about any of that, though, did she?

She smiled.

'That'll be all the tennis. You're just not used to it. If you play more often, you won't get so tired.'

'Mmmm. I suppose so. I think I'll play again tomorrow, and see how I get on.'

I turned over then, and snuggled under the duvet, trying to give her the hint to leave. Unfortunately, Mum was never very good at taking hints.

'And, Megan, I hope you're getting used to Alice not being around.'

I couldn't reply. This really wasn't a conversation I wanted to have at any time, and especially not right now with Alice lying under my bed listening to every single word.

Mum put on her softest voice. 'You just wait and see. You'll be in secondary school next year. You'll make lots of new friends. And in no time, you'll nearly have forgotten all about Alice. When you're all grown up, she'll just be a distant, happy memory from your childhood.'

I could feel the mattress moving slightly under my legs. Alice must have been pushing her feet up underneath it. She was making double sure that I wouldn't forget about her. It was a typical, reckless, but very funny Alice-moment.

I couldn't help it. I gave a sudden, huge laugh. Mum looked at me in surprise. I put my head in my hands and pretended to be crying.

Mum put her arms around me and rocked me. It would have been very soothing if I had been upset, but since I was trying to stifle my giggles, it wasn't very helpful. I made lots of gross snorting noises that I hoped sounded like sobs. Mum said, 'oh my poor darling,' and rocked me some more, while Alice's feet beat out a snappy little rhythm beneath the mattress.

Eventually I recovered my composure. I sat up straight, wiped my eyes and smiled a brave smile.

'I'm OK now, Mum. I just had a sudden sad moment. I was just thinking of what I'd say to Alice if I could see her now.'

While I said this, I slid my hand from under the covers and put it under the bed. As I did so I made it into a fist, in an effort to make Alice behave herself. Luckily it worked. The movement under my legs ceased, and I began to relax.

Mum got up to go.

'Better now? Call me if you need me. And remember, Megan, Daddy and I will always love you, no matter what.'

Great, I thought grimly. I'll keep that in mind for when you discover exactly how I've spent this week.

Mum kissed my forehead, and went out of the room. After waiting a few minutes, just to be sure, Alice rolled out from under the bed.

First I was angry with her but not for long, I could never be angry with Alice for long. Soon we were in fits of giggles and then we lay in the darkness without speaking.

It was nice, just knowing that she was there.

As I closed my eyes and dropped off to sleep I promised myself that Alice would never, ever be just a distant memory to me.

Chapter sixteen

Next morning I woke up to two distinct noises. The first was the sound of heavy rain beating down on the flat roof of my bedroom. The second was the sound of Alice snoring. She sounded like a pig or a rhinoceros or something. I listened for a while, and then decided I'd better wake her. If Mum happened to pass my bedroom door, she'd surely come in, wondering what the strange noise was.

I leaned down and shook Alice hard. She woke up and looked at me in surprise, as if she wasn't quite sure where she was.

'Megan?'

I grinned at her. 'Yes, Alice. It is I.'

She looked sad.

'Sorry. I was having a very vivid dream. I thought I was at home again. With Mum and Dad. And Jamie. Jamie was being really, really stupid. But it was nice all the same.'

She sat up straight and stretched her arms high into the air. 'But no more moping. Today we are thinking positive. Today is the first day of the rest of my life.'

I laughed.

'Yes. The first day of the rest of your life in Limerick.'

'Yes! The rest of my life in Limerick.' Her face took on that shiny, happy expression that I both loved and feared.

'Bit of a problem, though,' I added.

'What's that?'

'Listen.'

She put her hand behind her ear in an exaggerated listening pose.

'What? All I can hear is Rosie crying.'

Now that she mentioned it, I became aware of a soft wailing sound coming from the other side of the house. I hadn't noticed it before. I suppose I was just so used to it. It was the background noise of my life.

'I don't mean Rosie. Can't you hear the rain?'

'So? It's raining. Big deal. This is Ireland. It rains a lot here. Hadn't you noticed? Anyway, it's not raining in here is it?'

I sighed and wondered if she was deliberately missing the point. 'Of course it's not raining in here. But how can I pretend to be going to play tennis if it's still pouring rain this afternoon? Mum knows I wouldn't play in the rain. So how will I get out of the house?'

Alice clapped one hand over her mouth in an expression of sheer horror. I wasn't sure if she was faking it. With Alice it was often hard to tell.

She spoke in a hushed tone.

'You're right. This is a disaster. We're trapped. We could be prisoners for the whole day. It's not fair. It's cruelty to children!'

I laughed. 'Hey, it's not quite that bad. We'll think of something. Now, do you need to do some mountaineering before I go for breakfast?'

She shook her head. 'No. I'm fine. Ill wait till you get back.'

I shrugged, and pulled on my dressing gown.

'OK. I'll see you in a while. I'll bring you back something nice.'

Then, closing the door carefully behind me, I went back to my real life.

* * *

After breakfast, Mum said. '

You know what day today is, Megan?'

I pretended to think. 'Wednesday?'

Of course I knew perfectly well what day it was. Wednesday was an important day. It was half way through the week. Alice had been in hiding for two days, and we only needed to continue for two more.

Mum continued. 'Well, Wednesday is toddler group day. Rosie and I will be leaving in a few minutes. It starts at half ten.'

At these words, Rosie began to jump up and down. I felt like doing the same. Mum going out was an unexpected bonus.

Rosie clapped her fat little hands together.

'Yay. Toddle oop. Toddle oop. Bikkies. Juice.'

Poor Rosie. She had no freedom at all, and the only time she ever saw a biscuit was at toddler group.

Mum laughed, and stroked Rosie's hair.

'Well, Rosie's excited about it anyway. Why don't you come, Megan? You can play with the toddlers. You always like that.'

I shook my head.

'I don't think so, Mum. I'm a bit old for that stuff.'

'OK, you can stay here then. But no television and no computer. You can tidy the family room while I'm gone.'

I smiled my sweetest smile. 'OK. Leave it to me. Your wish is my command.'

Mum did her usual half-exasperated shake of her head, and then she went to get her coat. I did the good girl act, and began to stack the dishwasher.

As Mum was leaving she came back into the kitchen. 'Sure you won't come?'

'Yup. Quite sure.'

'OK, so. Be good. I have to go to the super-market on the way home, so I won't be back until about one.'

I had to bend my head over the dishwasher so she wouldn't see how happy that news made me. My hair fell down into a dirty porridge bowl, but I didn't even care.

As soon as Mum's car was gone from the drive, I skipped into my room.

'It's OK. It's me.'

Alice rolled out from under the bed.

I threw my arms in the air with a theatrical flourish.

'Ta-da! May I present you, Alice O'Rourke, with the freedom of this house? For two and a half long hours, you, Alice O'Rourke can wander the rooms of this dwelling without fear of discovery, or banishment to Dublin.'

Alice looked at me, puzzled. 'Quit the fancy stuff. Just tell me what's happening.'

'My mum's gone out,' I explained. 'We're free.'

Alice jumped up. 'Free, and starving. Take me to your kitchen.'

It was strange, sitting in the kitchen with her, watching her eat two bowls of Weetabix, and three slices of toast. She kept getting up from her seat, and wandering into the hall, as if she had never experienced such freedom before.

Then we tidied the kitchen together, and we worked as fast as we could to get the family room tidy enough to keep Mum off my back. After that, the rain stopped for a short while, and we played swingball in the back garden, where we were safe from neighbours' prying eyes.

When it started to rain again, we went back inside. I had a brainwave. I dug out an old vacuum flask from one of the kitchen cupboards, and filled it up with boiling water. Then I hid it in my room, so Alice could use it later, to heat up her noodles. I was very pleased with myself, and even Alice was impressed.

I wanted to listen to music in my room, but that wasn't really fair on Alice, who'd seen more than enough of my room over the last few days. So instead we lay on the floor in the family room, and we played Monopoly.

It was nice. Every now and then I was able to forget for a moment what was really going on, and for those few seconds, it was just like old times.

Sometimes I half expected, Alice to jump up saying it was time for her to go home for lunch, promising to be back within twenty minutes. Sometimes I thought Mum might just casually look in and offer us some wonderful treat like salt-free rice cakes or organic carrot sticks. Sometimes I thought Rosie would toddle in and sit on Alice's back, one of her favourite places. So sometimes during that game of Monopoly, I was very, very happy. And sometimes I was very sad.

I was being especially careful, checking my watch every few minutes, making sure it wasn't time for Mum to come home. It was only five past twelve when I threw a three, and landed on one of Alice's streets that had a hotel on it. She jumped up and did a triumphant little jig. "Pay up, sucker. You owe me fifteen hundred euro."

I was riffling through my money to see if I had enough to pay her, when to my complete horror, I heard a very familiar sound.

It was the distinctive, unmistakable

chug-chug noise of my mother's old banger of a
car pulling into the driveway.

Chapter seventeen

I went into instant, total panic mode. I stood in the middle of the floor and flapped my arms like a frightened chicken who'd been drinking too much Cola. This could be the beginning of a major disaster. To get back to my room, Alice would have to run past the glass front door and Mum would surely see her.

'Quick, hide!' I hissed.

Alice looked really pale.

'Hide? Where?' Her voice was all squeaky and scared.

I looked around the room. There weren't many choices. It was a small room, and Alice is a big, tall girl. 'Behind the couch, quick!'

She'd just hidden herself, when Mum walked in with Rosie in her arms. She sat on the couch.

'Oh, what a cross bunny this one is today. She must be teething.'

She looked at the game of Monopoly, still spread out all over the floor. There had been no time to clear it away.

'Megan, what on earth have you been doing? Why is that all over the floor?'

I sighed, hoping it would keep the panic from my voice. 'Oh, I got bored. I wanted to see if you could play Monopoly on your own. You can't, actually.'

That was a fairly weak explanation, so I tried to change the subject. 'You're home early.'

'Mmmm, I know. I couldn't face the supermarket with Rosie like this. I'll go later, after she's had her nap.'

Luckily, at the mention of the word 'nap' Rosie cuddled into Mum's arms and sucked her thumb. Mum got up slowly so as not to disturb her. 'I'll put her up now, poor little lamb.'

Mum had only got as far as the hall when the doorbell rang. 'Get that, will you, love?' she said over her shoulder as she went upstairs.

I went and opened the door. It was horrible, nosy old Mrs O'Callaghan from up the road.

What a treat!

Not.

'Mum's upstairs,' I said, hoping she'd go away.

She gave me a stern look. 'Why don't I just come in and wait then?'

She didn't wait for an answer. She swept past me and went into the family room, plonking her huge fat behind onto the couch. I winced. Alice must have felt the force of that.

Mum came back down. 'Geraldine. How nice to see you.'

Hah! And Mum gives me grief for telling lies. I

was convinced that she hated Mrs O'Callaghan as much as I hate Brussels sprouts.

Mrs O'Callaghan settled herself further into her seat. 'Well it's not a social call, Sheila. I'm here on residents' association business.'

I watched as Mum's face fell even further. Mum believed in changing the world. For her the residents' association was far too small and unimportant.

Mrs O'Callaghan wittered on for about half an hour about stupid stuff like leaves on foot-paths and whether parking should be confined to one side of the street. I sat in the corner of the room and pretended to read. I didn't feel it fair to abandon Alice even though there was nothing I could do to help her to escape.

Finally, Mrs O'Callaghan stopped talking. She stood up and went towards the door. Then she stopped and peered at Mum over her thick glasses. 'Do you ever see poor Peter from next door?'

I looked up from my book, alarmed. Peter was

Alice's father.

Mum shrugged. 'No, not that much.'

Mrs O'Callaghan took a deep breath, and then launched into a tirade. 'Well, that poor, poor man. How that despicable Veronica could just up and leave him, I just don't know. Of course she was always a nasty piece of work. I saw that the first day she moved in. Limerick was never good enough for her, with her designer-this and her designer-that, and her fancy Dublin ways. She thought she was better than the rest of us, and she's nothing better than a tramp. Good riddance to her, is what I say. We're all better off without her around.'

I sat still in my chair. I couldn't move. All I could think of was poor Alice, listening to these awful comments about her mother. If this was a horror movie, Alice would leap from behind the couch, launch herself on top of Mrs O'Callaghan, and scratch her eyes out. Fortunately for Mrs O'Callaghan, this was real life, and Alice stayed hidden.

I looked towards my mum. I knew she shared Mrs O'Callaghan's opinions about Alice's mum, but could I rely on her not to say so?

I held my breath. Mrs O'Callaghan folded her arms, carefully holding up her huge floppy chest. She too was waiting for a reply.

Finally my mum spoke. 'Well, Geraldine, I try not to judge others. I always found Veronica to be perfectly nice and polite.'

I could have run over and hugged my mum, but that might have aroused her suspicions, so I resisted. Mrs O'Callaghan unfolded her arms and rearranged her chest. She didn't like to be disagreed with. 'Well then, it's time I left, I'm sure. Goodbye, Sheila. Goodbye, Megan.'

She went out, looking rather offended, and banged the front door behind her.

Mum went upstairs to check on Rosie. I ran back to the family room, and hauled Alice from behind the couch. We ran to my room and closed the door behind us.

Alice sat on the bed. She wiped her eyes when she thought I wasn't looking, but I could see that she was upset. I put one arm around her. 'Don't mind that nasty old woman. She's only jealous. She's just a big ugly hag, and what does she know about anything?'

Alice shrugged. 'You're right. And I'm glad your mum defended my mum. It's nice to know that my mum still has some friends around here.'

I nodded. Luckily Alice didn't know that Mum only defended Veronica because she knew it would make Mrs O'Callaghan so cross.

Suddenly Alice looked really serious. 'You know what, Megan?'

'What?'

'I don't care what Mrs O'Callaghan thinks. I don't care what anyone thinks. All I care about is getting away with this for two more days. All I care about is making this plan work, and shocking my mother into moving back to Limerick.

That's it. That's all.'

She kicked off her shoes and lay down on the bed. 'Now what?'

I sat down beside her. 'I think we should stay in here out of trouble. I've had quite enough shocks for one day.'

Alice nodded. 'Yes, you're right. Let's stay here, and we'll have a nice quiet afternoon.'

Sometimes it's scary how very wrong you can be.

Chapter eighteen

It was about two o'clock and Al and I were in my room playing cards when the front door-bell rang.

Mum called from upstairs. 'Get that, Megan please, will you? I'm in the middle of tidying Rosie's room.'

I sighed. 'OK, Mum.'

I hoped it wasn't that old battleaxe Mrs O'Callaghan back with more of her nasty opinions. I'd had more than enough of her for one day.

I got up and went out into the hall. I could see two adult-sized figures through the frosted glass of the front door. Maybe Mrs O'Callaghan had brought reinforcements. Maybe she was going to use brute force to threaten us into caring about the parking situation on our road. Then I thought not. Even she wasn't that stupid.

It was probably political canvassers, I decided. Mum wouldn't be pleased. She always felt she had to argue with these guys, instead of just promising them all she'd vote for them, like Dad did.

I wondered if I could get rid of them without Mum knowing they'd ever been there. I rehearsed a speech in my head. I opened the door. And then I felt like shutting it again very quickly, because there, in living colour, on my front doorstep, stood Alice's parents. And they didn't look very happy. In fact they looked very annoyed indeed.

I looked at them and they looked at me. Then we looked at each other some more. I got a very sick feeling in my stomach. I wished I could be somewhere, anywhere else. At school. At the dentist. On the street being teased by Melissa. Anywhere would have been better than on my own doorstep, waiting for my world to crash down around me.

Al's mum, Veronica, spoke. Her voice was cold and sharp. 'Where's Alice?'

'Alice?' I repeated.

'Yes, Alice,' she snapped. 'My daughter.'

Alice's dad, Peter, gave a small cough. 'Our daughter actually.'

Veronica gave him an evil look, and repeated. 'Where is Alice, *our* daughter?'

I stood there for a moment with my mouth open. I couldn't think of anything to say. It didn't matter anyway. I was too shocked to speak. I opened my mouth and closed it again. No sound came out, not even the usual babble that pops out when I'm nervous.

Veronica continued. 'And if you're trying to think of a silly little lie - don't bother. You would only be wasting your time. We know she's here. Get her. Now.'

Her nasty tone convinced me that this wasn't a time for pretending not to understand what she meant.

'OK,' I whispered, and I went to my room. Veronica followed me.

Alice was sitting on the bed, pale-faced. Obviously she'd heard her mother's voice. Veronica's icy tones would cut easily through any walls. And when her mum spoke like that, Alice probably figured that hiding under my bed wasn't going to be much use.

She spoke weakly. 'Hi, Mum.'

Her mother didn't answer. She caught Alice rather roughly by the arm, and led her towards the front door. I followed, not quite sure what to do or say. As we arrived in the hallway, Mum appeared at the top of the stairs with an armful of dirty sheets. 'Who was at the door, Meg?' she began to say, before she spotted the four of us in the hall. She took a few steps towards us, and then she did something that really, really, annoyed me. She dropped the sheets on the stairs, and began to smooth her hair. I really, really, hated that. (Even though I'd often heard her mocking Alice's mum behind her back for all the time she spent on her appearance, Mum always seemed ill-at-ease, and almost shy in her presence. As if secretly she felt bad for not being as glamorous as her.)

And anyway, smoothing her hair was a total waste of time. Mum still looked like she'd been dragged backwards through a bush.

Then she embarrassed me further, by completely misunderstanding the scene.

'Veronica, Peter, how nice to see you. Hello,

Alice dear, have you come back for another few days? How nice. Megan has been missing you. Now, won't you all come in and have something to drink? We have some very nice herbal teas. They have no caffeine you know.'

Veronica looked at Mum as if she were a complete, raving lunatic.

'No, thank you, Sheila. This isn't a social call, you know. These two girls have been very, very deceitful.'

Mum looked at me. 'What exactly is happening here?' she asked.

I thought it wiser not to answer that question. Anyway, Veronica seemed happy to speak for me. She looked at Mum. 'I take it from your reaction that you didn't know Alice was here?'

Mum shook her head, and Veronica continued. 'Well, then it's even worse than I thought. She must have been hiding.'

Mum looked puzzled. She was normally quite smart, but on this occasion, she was very slow to understand what was going on. She spoke to Alice. 'Hiding? But....'

Veronica interrupted. 'She was supposed to be in Dublin with me, but instead she was here, hiding.'

Mum still looked confused. Then she nodded and gave a small smile as if she understood. Of course she didn't. 'Oh, I see, Alice. You were hiding next door, while your dad was at work. I suppose that was a bit bold. Your mother must have been worried sick.'

Veronica's face began to go a very strange pink colour, a bit like my strawberry shower gel. Only without the sparkly bits.

'No, Sheila. She wasn't hiding in her house. She was hiding in yours. It might be news to you that my daughter has spent the last few days hiding under your roof. Though how you couldn't have noticed, is quite beyond me'

Mum scratched her head vigorously. Great, as well as bad hair, now Veronica probably thought

Mum had headlice too.

Mum looked at me. 'Is this true, Megan?'

I nodded.

Mum scratched her head again. Veronica took a small step away from her.

Mum spoke. 'But why? You could have had Alice to stay if you liked. You only needed to ask. There was no need to hide.'

Veronica spoke coldly. 'I wouldn't have permitted it, Sheila. Her home is in Dublin now. Alice belongs with me. And I'd like to point out that I have a very busy schedule. I have lots more to do than driving down here to reclaim my errant daughter. I have to say this is all very inconvenient.'

That made me really, really cross. Alice's world was falling apart, and all her mother could think of was her schedule. She probably had to cancel a hair appointment or a session at the nail bar or something. I felt like hitting her, or stamping my foot or something, but since I was in enough trouble already, I just held my breath and looked at the ground.

Just then, Rosie appeared down the stairs. 'Alith,' she said, and she put her hands up to Alice, hoping to be picked up. Alice just rubbed her hair in a distracted kind of way. Rosie persisted, jumping up and down, repeating, 'Alith, Alith, up.' Mum picked Rosie up and cuddled her.

I put my head down. Suddenly it was clear to me that Alice and I had been wasting our time. Our plan was never going to work. There was no hope of her moving back to Limerick. Alice could have stayed hidden in my room for weeks, or even months, but still it would have made no difference. Nothing we did would ever change her mum's mind.

And then I started to cry. I knew that Alice had more reason to cry than me, but she just stood quietly between her mother and her father, saying nothing. I couldn't stop crying though. Big fat tears rolled down my face, and dripped onto my sweatshirt. I felt sad and angry and small and stupid. Mum put one hand on my shoulder, and squeezed it gently.

That small gesture gave me the courage to speak. I took a deep breath and the words came tumbling out. 'All we wanted was for Alice to come back here to Limerick. It's not fair. All her friends are here. Her dad is here. She's supposed to be at school here. This is her home. She shouldn't have to leave. It's wrong. It's cruel.'

I looked at Veronica. 'How could you do this to her? If you loved her, you wouldn't make her leave.'

I stopped then. I wasn't sorry I'd said the words, but I was very afraid at what would happen next.

Veronica took a step towards me. Her high heels clicked loudly on the wooden floor. She held up one hand. Her fingernails were painted with perfect black and white stripes. For a moment, I thought she was going to hit me. Then she stepped back again. 'You're two very

silly, immature, selfish girls. You only think of
yourselves.'

Just like you then, you nasty cow.

This time I kept the words inside my head.

Veronica spoke quietly. 'Come on, Alice,
come with me.'

With that she pulled Alice by the arm, and they
headed off down our garden path, and towards
Alice's house.

'Bye-bye, Alith,' said Rosie. But Alice didn't
look back.

Alice's dad, Peter, was still hovering awkwardly
in the hall. Mum looked at him. 'I'm sorry about
all this, Peter. I had no idea what was going on,
you know.'

He smiled, a tired kind of smile. 'Of course,
Sheila. It wasn't your fault, or Megan's I'm sure.
Alice is very strong-willed, you know. And the
move has been very upsetting for her. It's been
upsetting for all of us. We....'

He stopped. Then he smiled a sad kind of

smile. 'Well, thanks. I'd better go home and see what's happening.' I had a funny feeling he'd have been happier to stay there in our hallway, where it was warm and safe.

Mum spoke again. 'Before you go, Peter, please tell me one thing. How did you know Alice was here?'

He shrugged. 'I went to the tennis club for a drink last night, and one of the lads mentioned that his daughter had seen Megan and Alice on the Ennis Road, yesterday afternoon. Of course, I said he must have been mistaken, that Alice was in Dublin with her mother. But then Veronica phoned me at work first thing this morning, with a rambling story about Alice staying with me because she was sick. Well, it didn't take us long to work things out. She was rather angry - well, you probably saw that for yourself. She left Jamie with a friend and she drove down immediately. She's going back in a few minutes, I expect.'

Mum looked at me. 'Megan, has Alice left stuff in your bedroom?'

I nodded.

'Well, go and pack up her things and give them to Peter.'

I went without speaking. It only took a few minutes to roll up Alice's sleeping bag, and put her clothes into her bag. Then I grabbed a piece of paper and wrote a quick note.

'Bye, Alice. Sorry it didn't work out. Hope you're not in too much trouble. I'll miss you. Meg.

A few tears even fell onto the page, which was really sad, but I had no time to write a new note, so I shoved it under her clothes, and closed the bag.

Peter took the bag from me and left. Mum closed the door behind him. She looked at me, and said nothing. I wasn't quite sure how cross she was. She had a strange expression on her face that I couldn't read. This time, even she couldn't say, 'something just like this happened me when I was about your age.' So she said nothing. I thought about all the lies I'd told her over the past few days. I wiggled my foot on the hall mat. There was a hole in my sock. I couldn't help wondering if Mum saw it, would she want to darn it?

I said. 'Maybe I should go to my room for a while.'

Mum looked at me.

'Yes, maybe you should. We'll have a long talk about this when your father gets home.'

I went to my room, and lay on the bed. I could see the flask of hot water on the windowsill, all ready for Alice's tea. She wouldn't need it now.

After a while, I could hear voices from the front of the house. I went out into the hall and opened the front door. Alice and her mum were just about to drive away. Peter was standing on their front step, looking very serious. Then he turned around and went back into the house.

Alice wasn't crying, but she was awfully pale,

and sad looking. She looked up and saw me. She gave me a small wave, and I waved back. I could see her mum's lips moving, but Alice didn't turn towards her. She kept looking at me. We waved until they were out of sight, and then I went back into my room to wait until Dad got home.

Chapter nineteen

Much, much later I heard Dad coming in
from work. I heard Mum talking to him in
the hall, and then they went in to the family
room. They were there for ages. Dad probably
wanted to watch a match on television, but I figured Mum wouldn't have let him. I knew they
were talking about me.

After the longest time, there was a knock on
my bedroom door. It was Mum, Dad, and Rosie.

Great, I thought, a family conference. *Subject: How long should Megan be grounded for? All offers over thirty years will be considered.*

Questions for discussion:
1. Should she be allowed out for her confirmation?
2. Should she be allowed to watch television at any time between now and the opening ceremonies of the 2050 Olympics?
3. Should she be allowed out for her graduation dance?
4. Should she be allowed to have a mobile phone this side of her hundredth birthday?

I sat on the edge of my bed, and Mum and Dad sat on either side of me. Did they think I was going to make a run for it? Where would I go? Was I going to escape to Dublin and hide under Alice's bed until I was old enough to go to college? Hardly.

Rosie sat on the floor and started to play with my jewellery box. She emptied it out onto the carpet. I didn't care. I had more to worry about than my necklaces getting tangled or my earrings getting lost.

Mum spoke first.

'Have you anything to say, Megan?'

I hated that. Surely she'd discovered that tactic in one of those parenting books she was forever reading. I always felt it put me at a disadvantage in our discussions.

I decided to be brief.

'I'm sorry, Mum. Sorry, Dad.'

Dad looked me in the eye. 'Sorry? Is that it?'

I spoke again. 'Well, what else do you want me to say? I am sorry. Sort of. Can't you see? I only did it because I miss Alice so much. And she misses me. It's not fair. She should be here. Not in some stupid old apartment in Dublin. She belongs here, and all we want is for her to come back. Is that so bad?'

Mum spoke softly.

'Of course that's not bad. But you can't get involved. You can't change people's lives. It was a very silly thing to do. Her parents might have panicked. The guards could have been involved. It might have been a lot more serious than it was.'

Dad joined in. 'Her parents have to live their lives, and even though it makes you sad, there's not a lot you can do. It's tough, but sometimes kids just have to grin and bear it. That's just the way life is. You'll understand better when you're older.'

Mum and Dad had a lot to say. An awful lot. And it took them an awful long time to say it. There was a lot of talk about responsibility, and maturity and that kind of stuff. They weren't really cross, though. And they never raised their voices.

But after twenty minutes of meaningful discussion, I was bored out of my mind. In fact I was beginning to think that I'd prefer to be shouted at for five minutes, and given a proper punishment, and get it over with.

In the end, Mum and Dad decided that as a punishment I'd have to empty the dishwasher every day for a week, and vacuum the whole house every three days for a month. I looked at them in surprise. That wasn't much of a punishment. I did those jobs most of the time anyway. And more besides.

Mum and Dad stood up. Dad patted me on the shoulder, and said, 'Don't worry, Meggie.'

Mum gave me an intense kind of look. 'Sometimes you have to be seen to do something,' she said. Then they went out.

I puzzled over her words for a while, before a light went on in my brain and I knew what she meant. Mum and Dad needed to be able to say that I'd been punished, just in case they met any of Alice's family, and were asked how they'd dealt with the situation.

I smiled to myself. Maybe they weren't the worst parents in the world after all. OK, so in an ideal world, I'd have preferred ones who were a bit more generous with the chocolate and the electronic toys, and a bit less keen on vegetables and household chores, but I suppose you can't have everything.

After that we had dinner together. It was chicken with pasta, my favourite. As I ate, I found I was a little relieved that I wouldn't have to sneak back into my room afterwards to organise Alice's noodles. I was glad I wouldn't have to spend twenty minutes climbing in and out of the bathroom window. I was looking forward to just chilling out on the couch and watching TV with Mum and Dad and Rosie.

And then I felt really, really guilty.

Before bed, I asked Mum if I could check my e-mails. She nodded. 'OK, love, but don't be too disappointed if there's none from Alice. Her Mum is really very cross with her. She might not be in a position to be e-mailing anyone.'

Mum was wrong though. There was a

message. A big, long one.

Hi Megan,
   I've got good news and bad
news. The bad news is, I'm not
allowed to e-mail you for four
weeks. The good news is, Mum
plays bridge three nights a
week, and won't ever know if I
obey her or not. And Jamie's
asleep, so he'll never know
either so I won't even have to
bribe him to keep quiet. I hope
you didn't get into too much
trouble. I know I said I'd take
all the blame, but when Mum and
Dad showed up, I got such a
fright, I forgot all about it.
When we went into our house,
Mum really lost it. She was
shouting and screaming at me
for ages. Then the usual thing

happened. She started to blame
Dad, and she was shouting at
him as if I wasn't there. I
wanted to tell him to defend
himself, and not to let her
talk to him like that, but I
was too scared. Then, after
ages, Mum started one of her
'poor me' acts. She said,
'After all I've done for this
family, how could you do this
to me?' And then something fantastic happened - Dad went
really crazy. He doesn't usually get cross, but this time
he really lost it. It was scary
but great. He said all Mum had
ever done for the family was
ruin it, and that Jamie and me
are going to end up as delin-
quents, and it will all be her
fault. Dad really got going
then. He called her a big,

selfish social climber. He
said he was going to put his
foot down once and for all. In
the end it was really, really
great. I was so proud of him.
He said if Mum didn't promise
to let me and Jamie go to Limerick every second weekend,
and for half of all holidays,
he'd hound her through the
courts and have her declared an
unfit mother. Mum was quiet for
once. I think she got a bit of a
fright. And you know, she's not
as bad as Dad says. She just
needs more space in her life. I
think I can kind of understand
that. Then Dad made her promise that we can come down the
weekend after next, and guess
what? She promised. And I'll be
down for a full week at Christmas, and lots of times in

between. So you see, Megan, we won. It worked!!!!!! Thanks to you, I can spend lots of time at home, and even though it's not as good as moving back home for good, I think even I have to admit that it was very unlikely that that was ever going to happen. I was just dreaming as usual.

Thanks for your note. It made me feel both better and worse. But who cares? Let's look on the bright side of things. I'll see you in just nine more days, which is less than a week and a half away. And I won't even have to sleep on the floor, or eat dried noodles or climb out a single window.

Yippee!!!!!

Al

It was late, so I just sent her a short reply.

```
Al
  That is the best news in the
whole wide world.
Meg
  PS: You will never be a dis-
tant memory.
```

I wasn't sure about the last line. Maybe it was a bit OTT. But then I decided to leave it in. Alice and I had been through a lot in the past few days. I knew she'd understand.

I shut down the computer, and went to bed. Mum came in to kiss me. She even joked about Alice. 'Do I need to check under the bed tonight? Anyone else in the room, besides you?' she asked.

I shook my head. 'Just me, I promise.'
Mum hugged me, and then put out the light.
It had been a very long day.

Chapter twenty

It's the day after Christmas Day.

Soon Alice will be arriving to stay with her dad for ten long, lovely days. Her mum is going to Lanzarote, for a break. My mum laughed when she heard that, and said that it must be nice to need a break from bridge and tennis and going to the beautician's, but then she realised that I was listening so she didn't say any more. It wasn't a mean laugh though, and I didn't mind.

I'd better go back and give a quick account of what happened next.

Going back to school after mid-term was nearly as bad as September had been. But then, over the next few weeks, things started to improve. One day I noticed that Grace and Louise, two of Melissa's friends, didn't seem to be talking to her. I wondered why, but of course I didn't ask them. That night I e-mailed Alice to tell her. She replied that it was probably because they didn't curtsey low enough when they were talking to her. Then I e-mailed back and said that they probably forgot to admire her hair, or her new coat or something. Anyway, I didn't care what they were fighting about, it was nice to know that that there existed two more people who understood that Melissa wasn't the most wonderful creature on this earth.

Next day, Miss O'Herlihy decided to move our places in class again. She put Melissa next to

Jane, and everyone laughed. Melissa looked really, really mad, but couldn't say anything because Miss O'Herlihy had her very cross face on. Jane just sat up straight, and said nothing. I felt kind of sorry for her. (Not sorry enough to want to sit with her again though.)

Then Miss O'Herlihy put me next to Louise. I would have hated that before, but it turned out that Louise was really quite nice. At break-time she shared her crisps with me. And when I told her a joke, she laughed like she really thought it was funny.

A few days later, we were told to divide into three for history projects. Louise suggested that Grace, me and her would go together. I was delighted, but tried to look cool, like it was no big deal. We decided to do our project on the Vikings. We worked on it for two weeks. Grace and Louise came to my house most days after school, and we looked stuff up on the Internet. Mum made us celery and carrot sticks, and

Grace and Louise were really nice and didn't laugh once.

When the project was finished we all went to Grace's house for a pizza, to celebrate. It was fun.

At first, I didn't know what to say to Alice about my new friends. I didn't want her to be jealous. I didn't want her to think that I had already forgotten about her.

I needn't have worried though. She thought it was great that I wasn't on my own any more. She said that made her feel better about making new friends in Dublin.

One weekend when she was staying with her dad, Alice asked Grace, Louise and me over for an evening. We watched a video, and played basketball, and just did girlie kind of stuff. It was great.

That Sunday, when she was leaving to go back to Dublin, I felt extra bad. I told her so.

She gave a big laugh. 'Don't worry. I'll be fine. I'm invited to a sleepover in Dublin on Friday, and on Saturday a few of us are going to the pictures in the afternoon. I'll miss you. But I'll get over it.'

I laughed too.

She gave me a quick hug. 'And I'll see you the week after next.'

As her dad drove her away, I forgot even to feel sad.

*   *   *

So there it is.

I hope that even when I'm a grown-up, Alice will be my very best friend. Grace and Louise are nice, but they'll never replace Alice. We've decided that we both want to go to college together, and we're going to share a flat. Alice says she'll live with me forever as long as I promise not to feed her with dried noodles. I agreed, but made her promise to do something about her snoring.

Alice says she probably won't get married, after seeing how her parents turned out, but if ever she changes her mind, then she'd like me to be her bridesmaid.

I hope Alice and I will be very best friends when we're ninety, and shuffling round a nursing home in baggy brown cardigans and furry slippers, talking about hearing aids and walking sticks and stuff.

But in the meantime, I'm having fun.

Turn the page to read more of Alice & Megan's
adventures in

Alice Again

It's spring mid-term, and Alice has invited
Megan to visit her in Dublin. Megan is hoping for
a nice trouble-free few days with her best
friend. But no such luck! She discovers that Alice
is once again plotting and scheming.
Alice tells Megan that her mum Veronica has a
new boyfriend. She wants to find out who the
mystery man is and get rid of him. She involves
Megan in her plan, and Megan soon finds herself
caught up in a series of strange events ...

Chapter one

There was a sudden loud whistle, and outside in the corridor, I could hear the train doors whooshing closed. I waved at my mum and my little sister Rosie who were standing on the platform. Mum reached up through the open window and squeezed my hand.

'Bye Megan. Be a good girl at Alice's place,' she said. 'And remember, no silly hiding under beds this time.'

I groaned. Mum *never* lets me forget what happened last year. You'd think I'd robbed a bank or killed someone or sent a computer virus around the whole world or something really bad like that. But all I did was try to help my friend when she needed me.

You see, what happened was, my very, very best friend Alice had moved from Limerick to Dublin with her mum and her brother, because her parents had split up. Naturally, Alice and I were really upset about that, so when she came to visit her Dad at Halloween, she came up with this totally crazy plan. (Alice specialises in totally crazy plans!) She hid in my house for days, hoping that her parents would get such a fright that her mum would move back to Limerick and they'd all live happily ever after.

It didn't turn out that way, of course. Alice's mother wouldn't move away from Dublin, and Alice just got into loads of trouble.

Still, Alice's mum did let her visit Limerick a bit more often after that, so I suppose her mad plan sort of worked, in a funny, mixed-up kind of way.

Anyway, that was all ages ago, and everyone has managed to forget it except for my mum who has a memory like an elephant. Now it was spring mid-term, and I was going to Dublin to stay with Alice for six wonderful nights.

Just then there was a horrible screechy noise, and the train started to move. All of a sudden, Rosie started to cry. She stretched out one fat little hand towards me, and huge, sloppy tears began to drip down her face. At first I thought that she was crying because she was going to miss me, and that made me feel kind of proud and sad at the same time. Then I decided that she was probably just jealous because I was getting to go on a train, and she wasn't.

I put my face to the window. 'Don't cry, Rosie,' I called, 'I'll be home soon and I'll bring you back sweeties. Lots and lots of sweeties. All for Rosie.' Mum shook her head, and gave me one of her world-famous cross looks. If she had her way, sweets would be banned. Rosie was suddenly happy though. She stopped crying and beamed at me.

'Sweeties for Rosie,' she said.

I laughed. Rosie is cute – most of the time.

The train was moving a bit faster now. Mum lifted Rosie into her arms, and walked quickly along beside us. I wished she wouldn't do that. It was *too* embarrassing, and it's usually at moments like this that Melissa, the meanest girl in my class shows up, like I'm not embarrassed enough already.

The train started to go even faster. Soon Mum was almost jogging along beside it, waving madly. You'd think I was going to America for a hundred years instead of just Dublin for a week. Poor Rosie looked a little bit scared as she bounced up and down clinging tightly to Mum's neck. Mum's face was all red and sweaty and her hair-slide had fallen off so her hair was flying madly around her face. I wanted to shout out and tell her to stop making a fool of herself, and, even worse, making a fool of me. I couldn't do that though, I didn't want to hurt her feelings. All of a sudden I remembered that the dreaded Melissa had gone to Lanzarote on holidays, so at least there was no danger of her showing up and then telling everyone at school yet another story about my crazy Mum. Then I didn't feel quite so bad.

Mum began to slow down. I leaned out of the window and saw that she was running out of platform. Soon, if she wanted to keep going she'd have to run along an empty track beside the train. And even my mum isn't *that* crazy. At last she stopped running. She stood still with a very sad look on her face. The train kept going, and soon Mum and Rosie were like miniature versions of themselves on the faraway platform.

I gave one last wave, and then I sat down in my seat.

Free at last!

*   *   *

I could hardly believe it was true. It seemed like only yesterday that I was first allowed down to our local shop on my own. And I was only allowed into town if I spent half an hour promising to be good first. Now here I was, on a train to Dublin, all by myself. I felt like pinching myself to see if it was true, then I realised that was the kind of thing that kids only do in books, so I resisted. Instead I just sat back and smiled and smiled until I noticed the old lady sitting opposite giving me funny looks. I stopped smiling, and she went back to her knitting. She was making a jumper out of disgusting bright orange wool. It looked all stiff and scratchy. Some poor child would have to wear that, I thought. Now I had two reasons to be happy. One – I was going to spend six whole nights in

Dublin with Alice, and two – the knitting-lady wasn't my granny.

I put my hand into my jacket pocket and pulled out the e-mail Alice had sent me a few days earlier. I'd already read it about a hundred times. I read it once more, slowly, enjoying every single word.

Hi Meg,

I can't believe I'm going to see you so soon. And for six whole days!!! We are going to have the best time ever. EVER!!!!! EVER!!!!! I have it all planned. I've saved up loads of money and every day we're going to do something special. We're going to go to the cinema at least twice. We'll go to town and we can get our nails done in this great place I know. And there's a shop where you can design and make your own soft-

toys. I'm going to make a bunny for Jamie (you know how he loves bunnies) and you could make a teddy for Rosie. And there's this place where you can get the yummiest hot chocolate with heaps of marshmallows – it's all yummy and frothy – not a bit like the stuff you make at home. And Mum says we can go to this cool new Quasar place not far from our apartment. We are going to have soooooo much fun!

Luv

Al

I smiled to myself. I was really glad that Alice hadn't any crazy plans for this trip. Life always became very complicated when Alice went into what I called 'crazy-planning-mode'. I just wanted to spend a few days hanging out together. A few days free of organic vegetables, and Mum's efforts to save the world. All I wanted was a few days of fun.

I closed my eyes and thought of all the cool things that Alice had planned. Alice always had the best ideas. Suddenly I felt all kind of tingly and excited. This trip was going to be great. I just knew it.

I folded up Alice's e-mail and put it back into my pocket. There was another piece of paper there. I sighed as I pulled it out. It was the sheet of paper Mum had pressed into my hand as I boarded the train. I opened it up, and then I sighed again. It was like the ten commandments, only there were about a hundred of them, in Mum's ultra-neat handwriting, covering both sides of a very big page. Mum believes in lists – the longer the better – and this time she'd got completely carried away.

> *Don't talk to strangers.*
> *Don't forget to change trains at Limerick Junction.*
> *Help with the housework.*

Wear your coat when you go out – it's still only February.
Wear your gloves and scarf.

(I couldn't obey that rule even if I wanted to because I'd taken my gloves and scarf out of my bag when Mum wasn't looking, and hidden them at the back of my wardrobe.)

Don't eat too much rubbish.
If there isn't any healthy food, buy yourself some fruit every day.
Phone home at least once.
Don't stay up too late.
Don't go anywhere on your own.
Don't go out after seven o'clock.

The list went on and on and on. A huge long line of do's and don'ts. (Mostly don'ts). I felt as if Mum had climbed onto the train and was sitting there beside me waggling her finger in my face. I stopped reading and gave yet another big sigh. I knew Mum meant well, but sometimes she went a bit over the top. She badly needed to take a few chill pills.

I read quickly down to the end of the list just in

case she'd written something crazy and wonderful like – *I've hidden a hundred euro in the bottom of your bag,* or *I've arranged for a daily delivery of sweets to Alice's place.* (She hadn't, of course.) Then I tore the paper into tiny little pieces, and squished them into the small metal ashtray beside my seat.

I checked that the woman sitting opposite wasn't looking, and I gave another huge smile. Six whole days. Six days doing cool stuff with Alice. Six long, wonderful days before I had to go back to my own boring house, and all my stupid chores, and dinners with funny-looking beans in them. Six days of heaven!

It really was almost too good to be true, so I gave myself a small pinch, just to be on the safe side.

Chapter two

Despite all Mum's dreadful warnings, the journey passed without any disasters. I changed trains at Limerick junction, and I didn't talk to strangers, and I sat facing the front so I wouldn't feel sick, and I didn't touch the seat when I went to the toilet, and I washed my hands with soap and hot water, and I dried them on my t-shirt so I wouldn't have to touch the filthy hand-towel. I felt a small bit guilty about tearing up Mum's note, so I ate all of the carrot sticks and hummus and wholemeal crackers that she'd packed for me, and I didn't buy any rubbish from the buffet car. All in all I was the perfect child. Mum would have been proud of me.

The journey went very quickly and it seemed like no time at all until we were pulling in to the station in Dublin. I got off the train and followed the crowds of people, who I hoped would lead me to Alice. After a minute or two, I got to a metal barrier, and stopped. The crowd of people broke up, and everyone went different ways. I felt suddenly afraid. All my confidence vanished as quickly as jelly sweets at one of Rosie's birthday parties.

I looked all around and tried not to panic. There were hundreds of people in the station, but none of them was Alice.

What would happen if she didn't show up?

What if she'd forgotten that I was coming?

Where would I go?

What would I do?

For the millionth time, I hated Mum for not letting me have a mobile phone. Why did she have to live life like it was still the dark ages?

I could see a phone box at the end of the next platform, and I had some change in my pocket. Maybe I should go across and phone someone. But then I thought, who would I phone?

If I rang my mum and told her I was on my own in Dublin, she'd go into a total panic. She'd dial 999 and have the railway station surrounded by guards and soldiers and ambulances in minutes. I'd probably end up on the six o'clock news, and everyone in my class would see it. Someone would tape it to show to Melissa when she got back from Lanzarote, and then my life might as well be over.

And Alice never bothered to switch her mobile phone on, so there'd be no point in trying to phone her on that.

And I didn't know the number of Alice's landline.

A man with a huge battered suitcase hurried past me, knocking me backwards. I banged my elbow really hard on the metal barrier. It hurt like crazy. A lady gave me a kind look, and hesitated for a moment, but then she walked on. Everyone was pushing past me, busy with their own lives. Everyone except me had somewhere to go.

For one tiny moment, I wished I had stayed at home, where everything was familiar and safe. I could have gone to the pictures with my friends Grace and Louise, and then maybe Rosie and I could have baked an organic, sugar-free cake. I felt too young to be here in this big scary place on my own. It was stupid, I know, but I could feel tears forming, making my eyes go all blurry.

I was just reaching for one of the tissues that Mum had made me put in my coat pocket, when I heard a huge whistle that made all the people near me turn around in surprise. I smiled. I knew only one person who could whistle like that. Then I heard her voice,

'Megan. Me-e-eg! Here, I'm over here!'

I turned and looked, Alice was running along towards me, waving and calling. I quickly wiped my eyes with my sleeve, picked up my bag and walked towards her. I'd never in my whole life been so glad to see her. Actually I don't think I'd ever been so glad to see anyone.

Everything was going to be OK. The perfect holiday was just about to begin.

Alice gave me a little hug. Then she whispered. 'I'm so glad you're here. Something awful has happened.'

I stopped smiling. 'What is it? What's wrong?'

She shook her head. 'Sorry, no time to tell you now. Mum's waiting outside, and you know how impatient she gets. I'll tell you when we get home, OK?'

It wasn't OK, but I knew there was no point asking any more. Alice is the world champion at not telling stuff if she doesn't want to.

She took me by the arm and led me towards

the car park. Her mum's fancy car was parked right next to a *No Parking* sign. I smiled to myself. My mum would die rather than park there. My mum loves rules, and Alice's mum loves breaking them. I don't know how those two women managed to have daughters who were best friends.

Alice climbed into the front seat, and I climbed into the back. Her brother, Jamie, was sitting there, stuffing his cheeky little face with crisps. The seat around him looked as if a crisp-bomb had just exploded and there was a disgusting stink of cheese and onions. When I leaned over to close the door, Jamie kicked me on the shin. It really hurt, but I didn't want to say anything in front of Alice's mum. I made a face at him, and he stuck his tongue out at me, showing me a huge mound of gross, slimy, half-chewed potato.

In a way, I was kind of glad that Jamie was being his usual horrible self. At least the awful thing that Alice had talked about wasn't awful enough to make him change his behaviour.

I edged myself as far as I could away from him, and fastened my seat-belt.

Alice's mum, Veronica, half-turned around in her seat. She gave me the cold smile that always seemed a bit forced. Sometimes I thought she must practise it in front of the mirror. Maybe it was a special kind of smile that didn't cause wrinkles. My mum has loads of wrinkles around her eyes. Maybe she should learn how to smile like that.

'Megan,' said Veronica. 'How lovely to see you. I'm sure you and Alice are going to have a wonderful time together.' Veronica looked like she didn't really care if we had a wonderful time or not.

Then she turned away, and began to wipe some lipstick from her teeth with the corner of a tissue. Now I was really confused. If something terrible had happened, why was everyone except

Alice acting so normally?

Alice turned around, and gave me a small smile, and I felt a bit better. Maybe things weren't so bad after all. Alice was probably just being a bit over-dramatic as usual. She's good at that.

Veronica pulled out onto the road. There was a squeal of brakes, and a taxi screeched to a halt, just missing us. The driver leaned out of the window and shook his fist. He was just about to say something, when Veronica rolled down her window.

'I'm so dreadfully sorry. I just didn't see you.' I could see in the mirror that she was smiling a sweet smile. The taxi driver fell for it. 'No problem, missus. On you go.'

Veronica drove on, ignoring Alice who was pretending to get sick into Veronica's gorgeous white leather handbag.

Then Alice spoke crossly. 'Mum, that is so sexist. You shouldn't use your looks to get away with dangerous driving.'

Veronica laughed. 'That wasn't the slightest bit dangerous. He should have been more careful. Anyway, if I've got good looks, it would be wrong not to use them, wouldn't it? After all, Alice, you're brainy, and you plan to use your brains, don't you?'

Alice sighed. 'That is *so* totally different. I ...'

Her mother ignored her. 'And, Megan, you're good at ... Well, I'm sure you're good at something. And you'll use that to get on in life, won't you?'

I didn't know how to answer. Alice and her mum were always fighting, and I hated when I got stuck in the middle of their rows. Alice was my friend, and I had to be loyal to her, but if I made her mother cross, it could turn into a very long holiday.

Jamie came to my rescue. 'I'm good at lots of things, aren't I Mummy?'

Veronica turned around and smiled at him. 'Yes, my love, you are.'

He smiled back at her. 'I'm good at doing burps. I'm the very best in my whole class. Listen.' He did a huge, long, loud burp. The smell of cheese and onions became even stronger. Now I felt like throwing up. Alice giggled.

Veronica shook her head crossly. 'That's hardly something to be proud of, Jamie. You're good at lots of other nicer things.'

He grinned.

'Yes, I am. I can do rudies too. I'm nearly as good as Dylan. And I'm much better than Conor. Will I do some?'

Veronica turned around and gave him a fierce look. The car swerved, and I could see a huge stone wall rushing towards us. Just in time Veronica steered clear. The car behind us beeped loudly.

I sighed. Life with the O'Rourkes was never dull, that was for sure.

Chapter three

Soon we were at Alice's apartment. Jamie immediately parked himself in front of the television, and Veronica went into the kitchen. Alice brought me into her bedroom, and closed the door behind us.

I sat on her bed and picked up a furry purple cushion. Alice always has loads of cushions on her bed. (My mum says cushions are just holiday camps for dust mites, and doesn't let me have any.) I played with the cushion's silky fringe while I waited for Alice to talk. I was dying to know what was going on, but with Alice, it's always better to pretend not to be too eager.

After a moment she spoke.

'Mum has a boyfriend.'

I opened my mouth, but no words came out. What on earth could I say to that? A mum having a boyfriend just sounded too weird. Big sisters and babysitters and pop stars had boy-friends. Not mums. I couldn't picture my mum with a boyfriend. I couldn't imagine her with anyone except for Dad. It just wouldn't seem right. But then, maybe that's what Alice used to think about her parents before they separated. For a moment I was glad that my mum was all scruffy and worn-down looking. Surely she could never get a boyfriend even if she wanted one?

Alice stood in front of me with her arms folded. She sounded cross. 'Didn't you hear me, Megan? My mum has a boyfriend.'

I still didn't know what to say. I didn't have a whole lot of experience of this kind of thing. 'Oh

... em ... that's…. well ... I mean ... I'm sorry. I'm sorry to hear it,' I muttered.

Was that the right thing to say? Probably not. It didn't seem like enough, and Alice certainly didn't look very pleased. I racked my brains for some sensible questions. After a few seconds, they all poured out in a rush.

'How do you know? Did she tell you? Who is he? Have you met him? What's he like? Is he nice?'

Alice shook her head, but I had no idea which of my many questions she was saying 'no' to. She looked all worked up and sad. I patted the bed beside me, the way Mum sometimes does with Rosie. Alice obediently sat down beside me. I spoke softly. 'Just tell me everything.' At least if she talked, I didn't have to.

Alice took a deep breath. 'OK. Well, like I said, Mum has a boyfriend. She hasn't actually told me yet, but I know she has.'

For a moment I felt a bit better. Alice's vivid

imagination was legendary. Maybe it wasn't true at all. I spoke again.

'So how exactly do you know?'

She gave a sad laugh.

'Any fool could see it. He rings her every night. Always at seven o'clock. Just when *The Simpsons* is starting. It's been going on for ages. The first time I answered it, and it was a man's voice. Now Mum grabs the phone before Jamie and I can get there. Then she goes all shy and breathy, and she keeps fixing her hair, and she takes the phone into her room so we won't hear what she's saying.'

This didn't sound good at all. I spoke as brightly as I could. 'Maybe he's just a friend?'

She shook her head. 'No way. She hasn't got any men friends. And anyway, what friend phones every single night?'

I tried again. 'There's not much harm in phone calls, is there?'

She shrugged.

'Who knows? Anyway, it's not just the phone calls. I think she meets him during the day, when Jamie and I aren't here. When I get home from school she's always in her best clothes.'

I tried not to smile. It looked to me as if Veronica was permanently in her best clothes. She always wore really fancy suits to the supermarket, and once when she lived next door to me, I'd seen her putting out the bins in a long evening dress with sequins down the front.

Alice saw my look. 'No, really, Meg. I mean her very, very best clothes. And she keeps buying new stuff. And she's got this new perfume that she wears every day. And when I talk to her, she never seems to listen.'

No change there then. Veronica had never been a very attentive mother. Alice saw my look again. That girl was too smart for words. 'I mean she listens even less than usual. It's like she's living on another planet. Her mind is always somewhere else. She's gone all dreamy and moody. She thinks about him all the time. I know it. And she's got this fancy leather notebook, like a diary. I bet she keeps a record of all their dates in there.'

I wondered why Alice hadn't found the diary and read it. It was sneaky, but she could justify it by saying that it was for the sake of the family. Alice could justify anything if she tried.

She continued. 'I searched for the diary for days, but when I found it, it was locked, and I couldn't find the key.'

I decided to be brave.

'And what about your dad?'

Alice shrugged. 'What about him? Mum doesn't care about him any more, does she? And I know she won't get back with him. I know that's over forever, but imagine if she got married? Imagine if I had to live with her new husband. I don't want to have a stepfather. I have one dad, and that's enough. It would be awful. It would be ...'

She stopped talking, and I thought she was going to cry. At that moment I really hated Veronica. She'd messed up Alice and Jamie's lives. And even my life had changed forever when she decided to drag half her family off to live in Dublin. What on earth could I say that would make this better? Life had been so much simpler when my best friend's parents were living together and pretending to be happy.

I took off my coat, and as I did so, a piece of paper fell out of the pocket. I picked it up. It was Alice's e-mail. Suddenly I felt cross. Why hadn't she mentioned Veronica's boyfriend in her message? Why had she just talked about fun stuff? I was her friend. Why hadn't she told me the truth?

I handed the e-mail to Alice. She unfolded it slowly, and looked at it for a long time. Then she looked at me with a funny wrinkle between her eyebrows. She didn't say anything.

'Why?' I said, 'Why didn't you tell me about all

this in the e-mail? Why did you pretend everything's normal when it's not?'

'I was afraid,' she said.

I didn't believe her. Alice is the bravest girl I know. She's never afraid of anything. 'Afraid of what?' I asked.

Now real tears came to her eyes. 'I know you hate rows and stuff. I was afraid if I told you the truth you wouldn't come.'

I couldn't answer that. Maybe what she said was true. I felt kind of ashamed, even though I hadn't done anything wrong.

Then, all of a sudden Alice's mood changed. She gave me a huge smile. It was a smile that I knew very well indeed. It was a smile that made me very, very nervous. I held my breath and waited.

She jumped up from the bed. 'Anyway, I'm so glad you're here, Meg. Everything's going to be fine now that you're here. The timing's perfect.'

I felt even more nervous than before. I played

with the cushion strings so hard that I actually pulled a piece out. I hid it in my pocket, hoping that Alice hadn't noticed. 'What exactly do you mean?'

She smiled at me again.

'You can help me.'

I could hardly get the words out,

'Help you what?'

She spoke as calmly as if she was asking me to help tidy her room, or help her with her maths homework.

'You can help me to find out who Mum's boy-friend is.'

I allowed myself a small sigh of relief. That wasn't really so bad. In fact, it was almost harm-less. It might even be fun.

Then Alice continued, 'And once we know who he is, we can get rid of him.'

I thought I could hear a dull thud as my heart sank down to the pale-blue soles of my brand-new runners.

Chapter four

Sometimes Mum says that I allow myself to be bullied by Alice. (Well, actually she says that about twice a week.) I know what she means, but it isn't exactly true. Alice doesn't bully me – she's just very, very good at persuading me to do what she wants.

A while later, when Veronica was getting the tea ready, Alice took me back into her room to tell me the first part of her plan. As usual, she made it all sound very simple.

'Don't worry, Meg,' she began. 'You get the easy job.'

'Ha!' I laughed, 'Your plans never have easy jobs – just hard jobs and very, very hard jobs.'

Alice laughed too. 'Honestly, Meg, this time your job *is* really easy, I promise. This is all you have to do – at five to seven you just get Mum into the kitchen and keep her there while I go and hide in the wardrobe in her bedroom.'

I sighed. Last year Alice spent half her mid-term break hiding under my bed, and now she was planning to hide in her mother's wardrobe. What was it with this girl and hiding? Didn't she play enough hide and seek when she was small?

Alice continued. 'The phone will ring at seven, just like it always does, and when Mum goes into her room, I'll be able to hear every-thing she says. Then, when she comes out, you just distract her again, and I'll escape.

Couldn't be easier.'

I sighed. She was right. It did sound easy.

So why was I still nervous?

Maybe I'm just a chicken at heart. Or maybe it's just that I'm more sensible than Alice.

Once again I wondered why I'd agreed to go along with her crazy idea. I've always been kind of afraid of Veronica, and I really didn't want to get into trouble with her. Especially not when I was staying in her apartment, and couldn't just run off home if things got too rough. If things went wrong, I'd go to bed that night with Veronica mad at me, and I'd wake up the next morning and she'd still be mad at me. I couldn't escape.

And besides, I just wanted to hang out with Alice and have a good time. I wanted to do all the fun things she'd promised in her e-mail.

Maybe if I put my foot down now, and refused to help her, she'd abandon her stupid plan, and we could get on with our holiday.

But how could I be so selfish? This wasn't

about me. This was about Alice. It scared me to see how upset she was. She was completely changed from the happy, funny girl I used to know. I had to help her. If I wanted to be a good friend, I really didn't have a choice.

But still, something was sure to go wrong – I knew it. I just couldn't figure out exactly what it was.

I decided that I needed more information. 'What will I do?' I asked. 'How will I distract her?'

Alice shrugged. 'I dunno. Drop something and break it, maybe? I know! There's a purple vase on the kitchen windowsill that Mum really loves. She'll go crazy if you break it, and I'll have loads of time to sneak away.'

Typical Alice, always going for the dramatic option.

I shook my head. 'No way. I'm Megan, remember? I don't do extreme. And if your mum does go crazy, I *soooo* do not want to be the one who causes it. Any more bright ideas?'

Alice shrugged. 'No. Sorry. Anyway, you'll feel more part of the plan if you come up with the idea yourself.'

I didn't reply. Didn't Alice realise that I didn't really want anything at all to do with her plan?

She continued, 'Come on, Meg. You're clever. You'll think of something. Don't worry. It'll be fine. And anyway, if something goes wrong, I'll take the blame. I'll say you had nothing at all to do with it.'

She went on like this for a while, and in the end I promised to do as she asked. As usual, I wondered why I had even bothered to argue with her in the first place.

Tea that night was probably delicious. It was pepperoni pizza and chips and Coke and ice-cream with rivers of chocolate sauce dripping down over it – all foods that are on the banned list in my own perfect home. I couldn't enjoy the meal though – I had too much on my mind.

Veronica was quite funny, telling us about the first time she bought a pizza and didn't realise that it needed to be cooked, and served it to her family in an ice-cold slab.

Jamie was totally obnoxious, slurping his drink and burping loudly, and kicking the table legs. He probably would have kicked my legs too, but I was careful to keep out of his reach. My shin was still sore from his last kick.

Alice was being really sweet, saying over and over again how glad she was that I was there, and what a good time we were going to have over the next few days.

I couldn't concentrate on anything, though. All I could think of was what was going to happen after tea, when the phone rang. I watched in fear as the clock ticked rather too quickly towards seven o'clock.

When the meal was over, Alice and I helped Veronica to tidy up. There wasn't much to do. Interesting that after junk food there's so much less work. Less washing up must be good for the environment. I decided to run that by my mum as soon as I got home.

When the clear-up was nearly done, Veronica turned to Jamie and stroked his cheek, 'What about you, sweetness? Are you going to help Mummy tonight?'

Jamie made a face at her and shouted,

'No! Do it yourself poo-head.'

I couldn't believe it what I'd just heard. If I said that to my mother I'd be grounded for about a thousand years. Veronica didn't even flinch though. She just patted him on the head, and smiled, 'Maybe tomorrow so, my little lamb. Why don't you go and watch some television?' He grinned and ran into the television room. Veronica closed the door gently behind him and said, 'He's just tired, the poor little pet.'

Alice whispered to me, 'He's gone horrible lately, and Mum does nothing about it. She lets him away with everything. He's turning out to be the most revolting child in the world.'

I couldn't argue with her. I was already wondering if I would be able to stick his behaviour for the next six days. My sister Rosie was no angel, but she was a perfect child compared to Jamie. And she was only three – two whole years younger than Jamie.

A few minutes later, Alice nudged me, and pointed to the kitchen clock. I didn't need to look, but I did anyway. It was almost five to seven. Time for me to play my so-called small part in Alice's big plan. For one moment, I considered not doing anything. I could change my mind, and not get involved. But then I decided that would be really mean. After all, Alice was a child from a broken home, and how could I not help her?

I was just putting away the last of the cups, as the big hand of the clock ticked on past eleven. I suddenly clamped my hand over my eye, and gave a small moan. Alice giggled, but luckily

Veronica didn't hear her. Veronica stepped towards me. 'What is it, Megan? Have you hurt yourself?'

I kept my hand over my eye and nodded. 'Yes. It's my eye. I think there's something in it.'

She came closer, and spoke rather crossly. 'Take your hand down, so I can have a look.'

I removed my hand, and Veronica peered into my eye with her icy-blue ones. I'd never been so close to her before, and I wasn't sure I liked it. She had lots of thick black mascara on. It made her look a bit scary.

'I can't see anything. Come over here where the light's better.'

As I moved towards the light, I could see that Alice had vanished from the kitchen. Veronica peered into my eye once more, 'I still can't see anything. Alice, pass me a tissue, will you?'

Oh, no! Now what? If Alice had to come out of her mother's bedroom again, it would kind of spoil her plan.

I stepped backwards and blinked rapidly. 'Actually, Veronica, it's fine again. Whatever it was must have slipped out. But thanks anyway.'

She gave me a funny kind of look. 'Where's Alice got to? She…'

Just then the phone rang. I was so pleased with myself for distracting Veronica so well, that I suddenly felt brave, 'Will I answer that for you, Veronica?' I asked in my sweetest voice.

She pushed past me in her hurry to pick the phone up from the counter. 'No need, Megan, dear. I have it.'

She picked it up and pressed the green button. She put on the kind of voice my mum uses for strangers on the phone. 'Hello. O'Rourkes. This is Veronica speaking.'

I could just hear a deep male voice, saying, 'Veronica, how are things? Did you….?' Then Veronica pushed past me again, and went into her bedroom, closing the door firmly behind her.

Chapter five

It seemed like the longest phone call in the history of the world. I stood in the kitchen and watched the minutes tick slowly by. After about ten minutes, I tiptoed over to Veronica's bed-

room door, and listened carefully, ready to run off if the door opened. She was talking too softly for me to make out any words, but even through the door, I could hear the tone of her voice. It was just like Alice had described, all kind of sweet and breathy, like she was trying to impress someone.

I thought of Alice, hiding in Veronica's wardrobe, listening to what her mum was saying. It
must have been awful for her. But then, the
situation was pretty awful for me too. This was
all going to end in tears – I just knew it.

Just then, I felt something stick into my back. I
jumped and gave a tiny squeal. It was Jamie,
poking me with his dirty finger.

'What are you doing, Megan?' he asked.

Oh, no. Not much point sneaking Alice into
Veronica's room, if I was going to get caught
eavesdropping outside, was there?

I fell to my knees and pretended to feel around
on the thick white carpet, 'I dropped ten cent.
Do you want to help me look for it?'

He shook his head, 'No way. Look for it yourself, stupid-face.' Then he went back into the
television room and slammed the door behind
him.

I breathed a huge sigh of relief, got up and

went into Alice's room out of trouble.

Ages later, I heard the door of Veronica's room opening. I went out and met her in the hall. She was smiling a funny kind of smile, which vanished as soon as she saw me.

'Oh, Megan. There you are. Where's Alice got to? Is she in her room?'

I gulped. Would Veronica believe me if I told her Alice had gone to the shop, or something? Could I pretend not to know where Alice was? That was a bit pathetic as the apartment was tiny. Surely Veronica would never fall for the dust in the eye thing again? Was I going to have to break her precious vase after all? Where on earth was Jamie, and why didn't he oblige me with one of his world-famous tantrums?

Veronica folded her arms and looked at me as if I was a total idiot. I never felt that she liked me much, but ever since Halloween when Alice had spent three nights hiding in my house, Veronica had acted as if I was some kind of revolting disease to be avoided at all costs.

'Well?'

I gulped again, and tried not to look towards Veronica's bedroom door. It was right next to us, and there was no way Alice could sneak out without being seen.

'She's ... em-m-m ... what I mean is ... Actually, she ...' I was babbling, and I knew it. I stopped, and thought hard. *Distract her. How could I distract her?*

I backed into Alice's room. Veronica followed me. Veronica is the kind of person you'd be afraid of even if you'd done nothing wrong. If we weren't so high up, I'd have been tempted to jump out of the bedroom window and run away. I opened my mouth, and the words popped out all on their own, 'Veronica, I can't open my travel bag. The zip is stuck. Could you help me please?' As I spoke, I grabbed my bag from the floor, and shoved it towards her.

Veronica slowly unfolded her arms and took

the bag from me. The zip of my bag often *did* get stuck, but of course this time it slipped open easily. Behind Veronica, the door of her bedroom opened, and I saw Alice slip out, and into the kitchen. Veronica handed me back the bag, and gave me an even more scary look than before. Her voice was icy. 'There. That wasn't so hard. And now if you have a minute, you might tell me where my daughter has got to.' I smiled my sweetest smile. 'Of course, Veronica. She's just out there. In the kitchen, I think.'

Veronica gave me an evil look, and then spun around on one of her high heels, and walked towards the kitchen. Her heel left a deep mark on Alice's carpet. I went and sat on Alice's bed. I picked up the purple cushion and hugged it. I'd only been there a few hours and I'd already spent too much time cushion-hugging. It wasn't a good sign. I felt like crying. I was really, really sorry that I'd come to Dublin. Veronica was being so mean and nasty, and Alice was all wrapped up in her plotting and scheming, and Jamie was his usual totally horrible self.

Things were bad, and all the signs indicated that they were going to get worse. What about all the treats and fun stuff Alice had promised me? I was sure the week I had looked forward to so much was going to end in total disaster. It just wasn't fair. I might as well have stayed at home. At least there I wouldn't have expected any fun, so I wouldn't have been disappointed.

Just as the first tears came to my eyes, Alice came running in. She slammed the door behind her, and threw herself on to the bed next to me. She was all breathless and excited. 'I was right. I knew it. I just knew it. How could she do this to us?'

I pretended to sneeze, and used a tissue to wipe my eyes. I needn't have bothered. Alice was too caught up in her own drama to notice me and my tears.

'Norman. That's his name. What kind of a

stupid name is that? And Mum kept on saying it. It was "Norman this" and "Norman that" and "You're so right, Norman." I thought I'd throw up all over her wardrobe. Serve her right too, if I did. Stinky vomit all over her new Prada shoes.'

'Any chance he's just a friend?' I spoke timidly, fairly sure I knew the answer already.

'No way. She was all sweet and nice. Too nice for just a friend.'

'What kind of stuff was she saying?'

Alice thought for a moment. 'Well, not all lovey-dovey stuff. There were no yucky kissy noises or things. They probably save them for when they meet. It was all things like, "I did exactly as you said", and "no matter how I try, nothing seems to work." And then she kept saying how bold Jamie is being.'

'Well that's true, isn't it?' The words kind of slipped out.

Alice jumped up and stamped her foot. 'I know that. He is horrible, but I don't want Mum telling that to strangers. That's family business. And Norman's not part of our family. He's *never* going to be part of this family. No way!'

I spoke brightly. 'Still, if there was no lovey-dovey stuff, maybe everything's OK.'

I didn't believe that for one moment, but I just wanted to calm Alice down. Her cheeks were hot and red-looking, and her eyes were too bright and sparkly.

She shook her head sadly. 'The end was the worst part. Mum was quiet for a long time, and I could just about hear his voice, but not clearly enough to hear what he was saying. She just kept nodding and fixing her hair while he was speaking. Then she gave a little sigh, and said, "Thanks Norman. Your call means so much to me, you know. It's the only thing that gets me through the night."'

I gave a little gasp of horror. I wished I hadn't done that, but it didn't matter, Alice hadn't noticed anyway. She continued, 'And then, she said, "I can't wait to see you again. Tomorrow? Eleven o'clock. The usual place. "'

Alice sat down on the bed again, and put her head in her hands. She kept talking, but her voice was all muffled. 'The usual place. If they have a usual place, it must be really serious. Oh Megan, what on earth am I going to do?'

I patted her shoulder and said nothing. Once again I felt like crying. Because I knew exactly what she was going to do.

And I also knew that, despite my best intentions, I was going to do it with her.

Chapter six

And so, the next morning, exactly as I had feared, Alice and I were lurking next to a huge line of wheelie bins near the entrance to her apartment building. There was a disgusting smell of rotting food and dirty nappies. We were like two criminals in a very bad spy movie. Or the famous five, when three of them had the good sense to stay at home in bed. It was freezing cold, and I was glad I'd obeyed Mum and worn my warmest jacket. We'd been out there for ages because Alice had insisted on leaving early, in case her mother went somewhere else before her hot date.

Alice had told her mum that we were going to spend the day with one of her schoolfriends. Veronica had just shrugged and said, 'Have a nice day then, girls. See you later.' My mum would have insisted on phoning the girl's parents, and making sure it was OK. Still, I suppose my mum was right. Alice's mum didn't check up on her, and look what was happening.

Another ten minutes went very, very slowly by. My feet were going numb, and my hands were red and sore. My breath made huge clouds of steam in the cold, smelly air.

I tried arguing again, 'Al, I really don't think this is such a good idea. Your mum will see us straight away, and we'll be in the worst trouble ever.'

Alice shook her head grimly, 'She won't see us, because we're going to be too careful.'

'And what if she goes in the car? What will we do then? Are we going to run down the street after her at sixty kilometres an hour? I can run fast, but I'm not quite that good yet. Or is a taxi going to appear out of nowhere, and we'll jump in and say "follow that car" and the driver will shake his head and say, "kids these days" and race off with a big screech of tyres?'

Alice didn't even smile at my joke. 'Very funny. Not. I told you already. Mum hardly ever takes the car out. She walks nearly everywhere.'

I was cross and cold, and argued more than usual. 'But what if she's meeting this guy miles away? What if their "usual place" is at the other side of the city? Surely she'll drive then. And then what will we do?'

Alice thought for a moment, and then she gave me a bright smile. I felt that old familiar sinking feeling right at the end of my stomach. I knew the answer before she could get the words out.

'If that happens, we'll just have to call today a

trial run, and tomorrow, we'll hide in the back of her car before she leaves.'

All of a sudden, I felt even colder, and I hoped and prayed that when Veronica finally appeared, she wouldn't be waving her car keys.

The door to the apartments opened and closed about a thousand times. We watched loads and loads of people coming and going, but there was no sign of Veronica.

'Maybe she's not coming,' I said, after what felt like another hour. 'Maybe Nasty Norman phoned and cancelled. Maybe she's decided to stand him up. Maybe she's got sense and ditched him.'

'Or maybe he's got sense and ditched her'. I didn't say this out loud!

Alice didn't even look at me. 'No, she's coming all right. I know it. There's still loads of time.'

I checked my watch. It was still only half past ten. Unfortunately, Alice was right. There was still loads and loads of time. I wondered if it was possible to die of cold in Dublin in February. I wished my gloves and scarf weren't hidden away at the back of my wardrobe at home. I wished I had another few jumpers on, and maybe a nice woolly hat. An extra pair of socks would have been nice.

I looked at Alice. 'Aren't you cold?'

She shook her head, 'No. I'm fine.'

She was lying. Her lips were turning blue, and the tips of her fingers were white. I wondered if it was an early sign of frost-bite. Alice was very determined, but I doubted if even she would be prepared to sacrifice a few fingers just to discover who her mother's boyfriend was! This whole thing was crazy. I *had* to make her see sense.

I put on my most persuasive voice. 'Come on, Al. Let's forget about all this. I brought my purse with me. Let's sneak into town. We can go to that place you told me about. We can get hot chocolate. With marshmallows. And then we can go to the cinema. It'll be my treat.'

Alice looked at me closely, 'OK, so.'

I breathed a huge sigh of relief, and the cloud of steam that came out of my mouth almost hid Alice from view. I hadn't really expected her to give in so easily. It must have been the hot chocolate that did it. Or maybe it was the marshmallows. Alice always was a sucker for marshmallows. She even said that she could taste the difference between pink and white ones.

Then Alice continued, 'If you want hot chocolate with a big, fat pile of stupid marshmallows you go get it. And go to the pictures too. I don't care. You can do whatever you like. But I'm staying right here. I have a job to do, and I'm not leaving until it's done.'

Hot chocolate and the pictures wouldn't have been much fun on my own. And besides, Alice looked so sad. She looked all lost and confused and alone. I couldn't just abandon her.

And then for a second I thought how I would

feel if I were in her place – if my mum suddenly took Rosie and me to live far away from Dad and all my friends. And how would I feel if my mum started going on dates with a secret boyfriend?

And in the unlikely event of that ever happening, I knew that Alice wouldn't be all afraid and cautious like I was. She would do everything she could to help me. She wouldn't give up until everything was OK again.

I shook my head. 'No, Al, forget I said anything. If you're staying, I'm staying.'

She spoke more softly then. 'Really, Meg. It's OK. This is my problem. I should never have asked you to get involved. I've been very unfair to you. You go off if you want. I'll tell you exactly where to go. I'll tell you what bus to get and everything. I'll follow Mum, and see what she does, and I can meet you later. It's fine. Really.'

I knew she meant it. I also knew that she would stand there behind those stinky bins until she turned into a block of stone or ice or something. She could end up losing all her fingers and all her toes and the tip of her nose, like the poor guy I'd seen on the Discovery Channel a few days earlier. Sometimes Alice was too tough for her own good.

Hot chocolate would have been nice. I could imagine wrapping my fingers around a huge, warm mug, and breathing in the thick, sweet scent. I could almost taste the marshmallows melting on my tongue. But Alice was my friend, and she needed me.

I jumped up and down on the spot, and blew on my numb hands, and tried to smile. 'Who needs hot chocolate on a lovely warm day like this?'

Alice smiled back with her blue lips, and we waited some more.

Chapter seven

At about a quarter to eleven, the apartment doors opened again. Alice nudged me, and pointed. Then she hissed into my ear. 'Look. Here they come. Get ready.' Her breath in my ear was so nice and warm, I nearly forgot to feel afraid about what we were going to do next.

Veronica and Jamie walked slowly towards us. Alice grabbed my sleeve and pulled me further in behind the dustbins. The smell was even worse in there, and I could feel something soft and squelchy under my foot. I was afraid to look down to see what I had stepped on. Something revolting probably. I wondered why we couldn't have found a nice clean flowerbed to hide in.

I could hear Jamie's whining voice edging towards us.

'I don't want to go to crèche. I want to stay home and watch TV. Crèche is stupid.' Next I heard Veronica's voice, all soft and smooth and nice. 'It will be fun, Jamie. You can play with all your nice friends. And have some nice biscuits. Maybe there will be chocolate ones today. You love chocolate biscuits.'

'Don't want to go. Don't want to go. *Don't want to go.*' Each time he said it, his voice got louder and crosser.

By now, they were really near us. I could hear the clacking of Veronica's high heels. I was afraid to breathe, even though Jamie's whining would surely have drowned out any sound I was capable of making. I squashed even closer to a filthy bin. There was something brown and horrible trickling down the side of it. I tried not to wonder what it was. Through a crack, I could see Jamie and Veronica walking past. Jamie was making gross snivelly kind of noises, and Veronica was pulling him along by the arm.

Then, to my absolute horror, Veronica walked past the car park gates and over to her car. She took out her keys and opened the driver's door. Alice looked at me defiantly. I knew what she was thinking. She was already planning how we could hide in the back of her mother's car the next morning. I felt sick at the very thought of it. I closed my eyes and waited for the sound of the engine starting.

Then, I heard the car door slam, and Veronica's sharp tones again. 'Now Jamie, I have my umbrella, so if it rains we'll be nice and dry. Come on, darling.'

I let out the breath I hadn't realised I was hold-ing, and looked towards Alice. She was trying to look all cool and casual, but I knew she was relieved too.

I peeped out from our hiding place. Veronica and Jamie were out on the footpath outside the car park, and were vanishing around a corner.

'Quick,' I hissed. 'Let's go, or we'll lose them.' I was getting into it now, and didn't want to fail, partly because I knew that if this plan didn't work, Alice would surely come up with an even crazier idea for the next day.

Alice shrugged, and stepped slowly from behind her bin, dusting down her jacket as she did so.

'It's OK. No rush. They have to go to Jamie's crèche first, and I know where that is, so no point killing ourselves. And no point taking stupid chances. This is the easy bit.'

And so we walked slowly along the road, and while we walked, I wondered if every girl's life was as complicated as I had allowed mine to become.

After about five minutes, we got to Jamie's crèche. There was no sign of him, nor of Veronica. Part of me hoped that she had left already. Alice's plan was sure to fail, so maybe it was better if it failed sooner rather than later.

'I think we've missed her,' I said. I tried not to sound too pleased.

Alice didn't even reply. She grabbed my arm and dragged me into a clump of bushes just across the road from the crèche. There were no bins this time, but once again, Alice had picked a really smelly spot – there was dog poo everywhere. It wasn't fair. Starsky and Hutch never had to do this kind of stuff. I tried to find myself a clean patch of ground to stand on, and we waited. Again.

Before too long, the crèche door opened, and Veronica came out. She rummaged in her handbag, and took out a pair of sunglasses, which she carefully arranged on her head. Then she fixed her hair, dabbed at her lipstick with her finger, and set off down the road.

Alice leaned over and whispered, 'Now, Megan, let's take it nice and easy. Too close – she sees us. Too far away – we lose her. About fifty metres would be best. Gottit?'

I felt like laughing. What on earth did Alice know about trailing someone? When did she become the expert? Most likely all her knowledge, like mine, came from detective shows on television, and they probably weren't all that accurate.

Still, this wasn't the time or the place for an argument, so I bit my tongue, and edged out of the bushes with her. A woman wheeling a buggy gave us a very strange look, but Alice smiled at her, and said, 'We're just researching a science project for school. It's on urban dog poo.' The woman gave us an even stranger look, and hurried on.

I checked my watch. It was after ten to eleven. Veronica didn't appear to be in a hurry, so it looked as if her secret meeting place must be nearby. Alice and I sauntered along after her, and tried not to look too suspicious.

Then, just when everything seemed to be going well, Veronica took a sudden turn into a sweet-shop. Alice and I stopped and pretended to be looking in the window of a video shop a few doors down.

'Now what?' I asked desperately, 'She's hardly meeting the love of her life in a sweet shop, is she?'

I had a sudden thought. 'Hey, maybe she's going out with the guy who owns the sweetshop. If your mum marries him, you'll get free sweets for life. You'll have Mars bars for breakfast, and Crunchies for tea. Lucky you.'

Alice looked at me crossly. 'Yeah. Ha, ha! Very funny. Not. Anyway, I bet this is just a distraction. All we have to do is wait here until she comes out.'

'But what if she ducks out the back way, and

we lose her?

Alice gave me a scornful look. 'Why on earth would she do that? She doesn't know we're following her, does she?

I shook my head. Alice was right as usual. 'Anyway. I hope she hurries up. My feet were just beginning to thaw out. It's nice to feel my toes again – I missed them.'

Alice smiled at me. 'Yeah, mine too. And thanks, Meg. Thanks for staying with me.'

I shrugged. 'That's OK.' I could never be cross with Alice for long.

Alice touched my arm. 'Look, here she comes.'

Veronica appeared again, and we ducked behind a lamp-post. I was fairly sure that she'd have seen us if she looked our way, since we were two average-sized twelve-year-olds and we were trying to hide behind a single average-sized lamp-post. Luckily, Veronica didn't even glance in our direction. She was busy unwrapping a piece of chewing gum.

Alice grunted crossly. 'Huh! Look at her. She won't let me have gum, she says it's not suitable for young ladies, and here she is, chewing away happily.'

'Maybe she needs it. Maybe she's got bad breath, or something.' I knew immediately that wasn't a very clever thing to say.

'Yeah,' Alice said grimly. 'She needs nice fresh minty breath for kissing her fancy boyfriend, doesn't she?'

I could have kicked myself. 'Come on, Al. Leave it. Let's see where she goes before we jump to any more conclusions, OK?'

Alice nodded, and we set off once more on our slow chase.

Shortly afterwards, we came to another small row of shops. Veronica, who was still about fifty metres ahead, fixed her hair again. Even though it was still freezing cold, she unbuttoned her coat, and let it kind of float out behind her. She stood up straighter, and began to walk like the fashion-models on TV. I knew we were getting close.

Then Veronica took a tissue from her pocket, put her chewed gum into it, and tossed it into a bin. She checked her watch, flicked her hair one more time, and turned suddenly into a small, ordinary-looking coffee shop.

So this was it. This was 'the usual place', and Veronica's secret date was about to begin.

All of a sudden I didn't feel cold any more. I just felt very, very sick.

Chapter eight

Alice took my arm, and we edged along the footpath towards the coffee shop. It looked kind of ordinary. Not a bit fancy or anything. The writing over the door was grey and faded. There was a big long streak of bird poo dripping down the window. If I was going on a special date, I wouldn't have picked a place like that.

Alice edged forward again, until she had a good view in through the window. I huddled behind her. I really didn't want to know what was going on inside. That didn't matter though – I knew I could rely on Alice to fill me in on all the gory details.

'I can see her,' she hissed. 'She's in the queue.' I fervently wished that Veronica could behave like a normal mum. Just this once. I wished she'd have a nice quiet cup of coffee on her own, and then go home and do the ironing or something. And then Alice and I could forget about all this spying stuff and enjoy our day.

No such luck though. Alice edged forwards even more, talking all the time. 'She's nearly at the till now. She's got a tray. And ...'

'And what?' I forgot I wasn't supposed to be interested.

Alice's voice was flat, 'And she's got two cups.'

I didn't even bother hoping that Veronica was really thirsty and needed two cups of coffee, or that she was meeting a woman friend for a nice chat. I knew this was serious.

I edged in even further behind Alice. 'Can you see the tables? Can you see any men sitting on their own?'

She leaned forwards. 'I don't think so. It's mostly women. The place is full of housewives. It's housewife heaven.'

I didn't even get a chance to laugh, as she continued. 'Oh, no! There is one man there.'

I couldn't bear to look. 'Is he on his own?'

She nodded. 'So far. But Mum's still in the queue. Maybe he's waiting for her to join him. But no. He couldn't ... I mean she couldn't ... He's ...'

'What is it?'

'Look, Meg. Look at the guy sitting there next to the plant.'

I leaned around her and looked. And then I looked some more.

Surely this wasn't Norman?

This couldn't possibly be Alice's future stepfather?

Or could it?

He was a tall, pale, skinny-looking man. He had only one long piece of hair, and it was stretched across the top of his head – maybe he hoped no-one was going to notice that apart from this greasy, stringy thing, the top of his head was completely bald. He was wearing a really shiny grey suit and dirty runners. He was eating a giant doughnut. There was a line of gooey cream all around his mouth. As I watched, he took out a hanky, blew his nose, and then used the same hanky to wipe his mouth. I tried not to shudder. I glanced at Alice. She had been pale to start with, but now her skin was the horrible yellowy-white colour of the smelly cheese my mum buys at the market on Saturdays.

Alice whispered, 'Mum wouldn't. She ...'

All of a sudden, I knew she was right. Veronica would never fall for a guy like that. He just wasn't her type. She was too into clothes and appearances and all that kind of stuff. She would never go out with someone who didn't dress well, or who didn't know how to use a hanky properly.

My mum, now, she might go for someone like him, if she thought he was a good person, or had strong views on the environment, but Veronica? Never.

I grinned at Alice,

'Don't worry, Al. Not even in your worst nightmares.'

She grinned back, 'I suppose you're right.'

Just when I was beginning to breathe a small sigh of relief, Alice grabbed my arm again. It hurt. Why did she keep grabbing my arm anyway? Her fingers were stronger than she realised. I had a funny feeling my arm was going to be black and blue before the end of that day.

'Look, Meg. I bet that's him. That's the kind of guy my mum would like.' She was hissing again. She was pointing to a man who was standing on the edge of the footpath, just across the road from us. He was young. Well, younger than Veronica that's for sure. He was wearing a really nice jacket and trousers, and he was carrying a smart leather briefcase. His hair was gelled up a bit in the front, but not so much as to make him look like a wannabe teenager. Just enough to make him look a little bit cool.

Suddenly the traffic cleared, and the man crossed the road, ending up right beside us. Alice and I put our heads down and pretended to be very interested in the cracks in the footpath. We watched the man's feet walking away from us. They were nice feet actually, not too big and not too small, and he had quite cool blue shoes on. Keeping my head down, I watched the shoes walk towards the coffee shop. Seconds later, I got a waft of expensive-smelling aftershave. I hadn't a whole lot of experience of that kind of thing, but I had a feeling he smelled exactly like a guy who was going on a special date.

'Do you think that's him?' I asked.

Alice sighed. 'Only one way to find out.' Then without warning she called out loudly, 'Norman!'

The man turned around, but as he did so, Alice grabbed me and dragged me into a doorway. 'It's him all right,' she said.

I rubbed my arm, and peeped around the corner. Norman was looking all around him, probably wondering why, on a seemingly empty street, someone was calling his name. Then he gave a small shrug, and stepped inside the coffee shop.

Alice stayed hidden in the doorway, with a really cross expression on her face. I had to look though. I had to know. I leaned forwards, and watched, as the man stood inside the door of the coffee shop and looked around. If it was a pantomime, I could have had great fun shouting – *'she's behind you.'* This was no pantomime though, and I was quite sure it wasn't going to have a happy ending.

By now, Veronica was sitting at a table by the window. I had a perfect view. Her coat was carefully folded on a chair beside her. She was fiddling with her necklace with one hand, and with the fingers of her other hand she was tapping the table. She didn't usually do that kind of thing – it was too bad for her false nails. She must have been very nervous.

Then she looked up and saw Norman. She fixed her hair – again. She smiled and waved. Norman walked towards her. She half got up, and held her hand out to him. He took her hand in both of his, like guys do on the telly when they are trying to look really sincere. She smiled at him some more, like she was the happiest woman on earth. He was turned away from me, so I couldn't see if he was smiling back at her. He probably was. I glanced at Alice. She was still examining the cracks in the footpath. By now she could have drawn a perfect picture of them for art class. Anyway, maybe it was best that she didn't see what was going on.

I looked back inside the coffee shop. Norman was still holding Veronica's hand. This must have been the longest handshake in history. And then disaster struck. Norman leaned forwards and kissed Veronica on the cheek.

I felt like sitting down on the hard, cold, cracked footpath and crying until a huge river of my tears could wash me somewhere far, far away from this awful place.

Chapter nine

Of course I didn't want to tell Alice exactly what I had seen. So she had to persuade me. That took about twenty-two seconds. Impressive – even for Alice.

She listened carefully to what I said. She didn't scream or shout or stamp her foot or anything. She didn't threaten to run in and ask Norman what business he had kissing her mother. She was quiet, which really, really scared me. Cross I could have coped with, or sulky even, but quiet was just too strange and too hard to deal with.

We walked slowly back to her place. Alice went straight to her room and lay on the bed and looked at the ceiling. I went into the kitchen and made hot chocolate. I stirred and stirred but I couldn't get it all nice and frothy like they do in coffee shops. I floated lots of tiny pink marshmallows on top. Then I rummaged in the cupboards until I found some chocolate biscuits. I set a tray as nicely as I could. I wasn't sure it would help, but I couldn't think of anything else to do.

I carried everything into Alice's room. She said 'thanks', but she put the hot chocolate on the floor without drinking it. She didn't take a biscuit, so I knew things were really bad. Alice loves chocolate biscuits as much as my mum loves organic porridge.

Alice lay and looked at the ceiling some more. I sipped my drink, and wondered what I'd have been doing if I was at home. Not drinking hot chocolate and eating chocolate biscuits of course, but still, I had a feeling it would have been better than this. Anything would have been better than this. I wanted to help Alice, to make everything better, but I didn't know how. When chocolate biscuits failed, I was all out of ideas.

I hated all this serious stuff. All I wanted was to have some fun with my very best friend. Was that too much to hope for?

After ages and ages, Alice spoke. Her voice was quiet and hoarse, almost as if she'd forgotten how to speak. Maybe she had – I'd never known her to be so quiet for so long.

'You're sure he actually kissed her?'

I sighed. 'Yes, I'm sure. But he didn't go anywhere near her lips, I promise. It was only on the cheek.'

Alice's voice was getting stronger. 'And your point is?'

'Maybe he's just a friend. Lots of friends kiss when they meet these days. It's what adults do. I bet they're just friends.'

I didn't believe this of course, and I wondered for the hundredth time why I had told her about the stupid kiss in the first place. It was the shock that did it, I suppose.

Alice ignored me. 'I wonder how long before she tells us about him? I wonder how long before she brings him home?'

Then she put on her mother's voice. '*Children, I want you to meet Norman, my very special friend.*'

Alice rolled on to her tummy, and punched her pillow. 'She can't do this to us. She just can't. I am *so* not going to let this happen.'

I wasn't very comfortable with this kind of fighting talk. Why couldn't Alice just accept bad stuff? Why did she always think she could change things?

I spoke as softly as I could. 'Maybe it's not so bad. Maybe you'll get used to it. Other kids do.'

Alice sat up and stared at me. 'Well I'm not "other kids". I'm never going to get used to it. I'm

never going to like him. I'm never going to talk
to him. I am *not* going to let him barge in here
messing up my family. I'm going to– '

She stopped suddenly.

I looked at her carefully. 'You're going to
what?'

She smiled, but she didn't answer my question.
'Come on, Al. Tell me. What are you going to
do?' Once again I was asking a question that I
didn't want to hear the answer to.

Alice smiled again. 'It's just come to me. Now I
know exactly what I am going to do.'

'And that is?'

She smiled an even bigger smile. 'I'm going to
be so weird, and so horrible, and so demanding,
that Norman won't want anything to do with
Mum any more. I'm going to scare him out of
our lives forever.'

Oh, no! All kinds of horrible scenarios opened
themselves up before me. This could become
very unpleasant indeed. I wanted to help Alice,

but this could never work. She'd just end up in heaps of trouble. I had to find a way of stopping her before things turned nasty.

'But your mum isn't stupid. She'll know what you're doing. She won't let you away with it. She'll kill you.'

I wasn't joking. I'd seen how cross Veronica could get over a broken fingernail. I could hardly bear to think how wild this would make her.

Alice shrugged. She spoke breezily. 'She might be a small bit cross at first.'

I gasped, 'A small bit?'

Alice made a face. 'OK, so maybe she'll be very cross, but she'll thank me in the long run. I'll be doing her a favour really. She just won't realise it at first.'

She leaned down and picked up her hot chocolate from the floor. By now it must have been cold chocolate, but Alice didn't seem to mind. She drank it all in one huge gulp. Then she wiped her mouth, folded her arms and said,

'Tomorrow. I'll start tomorrow. Now, what do you think we should do first?'

*   *   *

Twenty minutes later, Alice and I were sitting on the floor of the living room, huddled over a huge medical dictionary. It was the grossest book I had ever seen. There were completely revolting pictures in it – pictures that surely should have had an '18' rating. They weren't suitable for my sensitive eyes, that was for sure.

We had already rejected scarlet fever, mumps and impetigo. These would have been impressive, but we figured they'd be a bit hard to fake.

I was getting really fed up, and some of the pictures were making me feel a bit sick. I knew I'd have nightmares that night, dreaming of horrible scabby things growing all over my body. I grabbed the book, and flicked quickly through it. Then I turned the page back to *Appendicitis*.

I pointed as I held the book towards Alice. 'There. That's the one.'

She took the book from me and read it. 'Hmmm. Not very original, is it?'

I felt like punching her. Alice is lucky I'm not an aggressive kind of girl. 'It doesn't *have* to be original, Al. This isn't a creative writing competition. We don't want original. We want boring, but convincing.'

She shrugged. 'Yeah, maybe you're right. Let's see, what do I need to do?'

She ran her finger down the list of symptoms. 'Pain in lower right side of abdomen, loss of appetite, nausea, foul breath. Yeah, think I can manage all of those.'

She slammed the book closed, and replaced it on the shelf. 'That's settled then. Tomorrow morning, between nine and ten o'clock, I am going to get a severe attack of appendicitis.'

I still wasn't happy with the plan. I had only suggested appendicitis to stop Alice from deciding on something even more drastic. If I hadn't stepped in, she'd have tried to fake a broken leg, or something. Or even worse, she might have really broken her leg. When Alice is determined, she never knows when to stop.

'Al, I'm not sure about this at all. Even if your mum falls for it, what happens then?'

'She has to miss her date with Norman.'

'So what? What difference does that make? She rings him up and tells him she can't come because you're sick, and then she arranges to meet him the next day instead. Big deal. That will hardly scare him away, will it? Or do you plan to fake appendicitis every morning for the rest of your life?'

'Of course not, dork-head. It's just that Norman probably doesn't have kids – he looks too clean to be a dad. I want to show him what a pain we are. Kids always mess up adults' plans. That's what we're best at. Norman will soon get the message. Then he'll ditch Mum and go and find himself a nice, child-free girlfriend. He's a good-looking guy, he doesn't need to be stuck with Mum and Jamie and me.'

I sighed. I knew that this wouldn't turn out to be as simple as Alice expected. Nothing ever did.

'OK. So you pretend to be sick, and your mum cancels her date tomorrow. Then what happens?'

Alice smiled brightly. 'Oh, I haven't decided yet. Something horrible though, that's for sure.'

The sick feeling that hit my stomach right then wasn't one bit fake.

Chapter ten

That night, as I had feared, nightmares from the medical encyclopaedia kept waking me up. At one stage I was dreaming that one of my eyes was all purple and puffed up like a basketball. I must have been crying out in my sleep, because Alice threw one of her cushions at me and snapped me out of it. It didn't help though, because when I went back to sleep, the dream was still there, waiting for me. The night continued like that until Alice finally ran out of cushions, and I slept restlessly on through my nightmares until morning came.

Anyway, after all that, I was really tired in the morning. I lay on the spare bed in Alice's room with my eyes closed. How I wished that I had a normal day to look forward to – a trip to town, or maybe to the cinema. Even a day tidying the apartment would have been better than Alice's plan.

Still, maybe Alice had got sense in the night and decided that her plan wasn't going to work. Maybe I was going to have a real holiday after all.

No chance of that though. Alice shook me out of my daydreams. 'Get up, Meg. Get up,' she said. 'We have a plan to put into action. Remember?'

How could I have forgotten?

I didn't bother arguing. I just got dressed and followed Alice into the kitchen. Veronica and Jamie were sitting at the table. I helped myself to a huge bowl of cereal. I didn't even bother to look at the packet – anything that wasn't porridge was fine by me. Alice sat next to me. She didn't take any cereal at all, and I could see that she was trying to look sick. Veronica didn't notice though. She was too busy seeing to Jamie's endless whims.

'I want sugar.'

'But, darling. There's sugar in that cereal already. Look, it says so on the packet.'

'I *want sugar.*'

'OK, darling. Here's some.' She poured a spoon of sugar over his cereal.

'I want *more* sugar ...'

'But, darling ...'

'*I want more sugar, dummy-head!*'

Veronica patted his hand. 'OK, darling. Here's some more, because you're such a good boy.'

Hello?? What planet was she hanging out on? When was Jamie ever a good boy?

Alice made a face at me, and I made one back at her. Even when they lived in Limerick, Jamie had always been a bit of a pain, but now he was completely horrible.

Alice gave a big, loud, exaggerated sigh, but still Veronica didn't notice. She was too busy trying to stop Jamie from pouring yet another spoon of sugar into his bowl.

Alice gave a huge, theatrical moan. At last Veronica looked up. 'What on earth was that awful noise?'

Alice leaned forward and held her stomach. 'It's me, Mum. I don't feel well at all.'

Veronica made an impatient clicking kind of noise with her tongue, and then she got up, and walked around the table towards us. Jamie saw his opportunity. He put his hand into the sugar bowl, and grabbed a fistful of sugar, and tried to pour it into his mouth. The sugar streamed down over his clothes, across the table and down onto the floor. Jamie looked in surprise at his empty fist. Then he took his milky spoon from his cereal and dipped it into the sugar. In a matter of seconds he had stuffed three huge heaped spoons of sugar into his bold little face. My mum says that sugar gives you worms. If she's right, it looks like Jamie will be able to set up his own worm farm some time very soon.

Veronica put her hand on Alice's forehead. 'You don't feel hot.'

Alice moaned again. I thought she was going a bit over the top, but Veronica didn't seem to notice. 'Have you a pain somewhere?'

Alice nodded weakly. 'Yes, right here.' She put her hand on her left side. She never had been very good about right and left. Luckily, Veronica had looked away for a moment, so I shook my head at Alice, and pointed, and she put her hand on the other side.

Veronica smiled at her, 'Maybe you're just a bit constipated.'

Yuck. I really didn't want to be part of this conversation.

Alice shook her head a bit fast for someone who was supposed to be so sick. 'No, Mum. It's not that. It's a really, really, reeeeally bad pain.' As she spoke she leaned forwards even more and gave a fairly good impression of someone who was about to roll over and die.

Veronica suddenly saw what Jamie was doing. 'Jamie, stop that, please,' she said, very crossly. Jamie ignored her of course. By now the sugar bowl was almost empty so it didn't really matter anyway.

Veronica turned back to Alice and patted her arm. 'Alice love, why don't you go and lie down for a while?'

Alice nodded weakly, and left the room, grabbing a bulb of garlic from the vegetable rack as she did so.

I followed her. 'What on earth is the garlic for?'

'Pay attention, Megan. Remember the book said if you have appendicitis you have bad breath too? And there's nothing better than garlic for foul breath, is there?'

I didn't think that was exactly what the book meant by foul breath, but I wasn't in the mood for arguing. I was just too tired.

Alice sat on her bed, and used her fingernails to peel the skin from two huge cloves of garlic. Then she shoved them into her mouth, and chewed, making a horrible face as she did so. She gulped and swallowed, then leaned towards me,and breathed in my face. 'Bad enough?'

I jumped backwards. 'Yes! Revolting! Truly gross.'

She shoved the garlic skins under the bed, and then jumped into it, and pulled the covers over her, and practised looking weak. I sat on the bean-bag, and we waited. And waited. And waited. Outside, we could hear endless rows, as Jamie threw tantrums, and Veronica tried to console him. I heard the sound of something breaking on the kitchen tiles – probably the sugar bowl. Much, much later, Veronica put her head around the bedroom door. She had her make-up on, and her hair was all neat and tidy.

'How are you feeling now, darling?'

Alice clutched her stomach. 'Oh, I'm worse, Mum. Much worse.'

Veronica went over and sat on the bed. 'Phew. What is that smell? Your breath smells foul.'

She turned away for a second and Alice gave me a thumbs-up sign. I wasn't brave enough to do one back to her.

Veronica leaned towards her again. 'You smell of garlic. But why on earth would you smell of garlic? We haven't had garlic all week.'

Alice gave a weak little shrug. 'I don't know. Maybe it's something to do with being sick. I wonder what kind of sickness gives you foul breath?'

Veronica patted her on the head. 'How would I know? I'm not a doctor. Anyway, darling, I have to go out in a little while. I have a few things to do. You'll be OK here with Megan, won't you?'

Alice shook her head violently. 'No, Mum,

don't leave me. The pain's very bad. Don't go, please don't go. Don't leave me.' She grabbed her mother's hand and squeezed it hard.

Veronica looked puzzled. 'This came on very quickly.'

Alice gave a small cough. 'I know, but Mum ...' She stopped and held her stomach again, moaning loudly. I knew she was faking, but even so, it was very, very convincing. Alice had always been the best in our class at acting.

Veronica got up from the bed. 'I'll just drop Jamie to his crèche, then, I'll only be gone for a few minutes.'

We had expected this. Alice had decided that if Veronica went to drop Jamie off, she'd get the opportunity for a few sneaky moments with Norman before she got back. For the plan to work though, they had to be kept apart altogether. Norman had to think that Veronica was totally trapped by her kids, and couldn't escape for the smallest moment.

Alice doubled over in the bed, and moaned even louder than before. I wondered how thin the walls were, and if the neighbours would start complaining.

Then she popped her head up. Her hair was all over her face. She spoke in a thin, whiny voice. 'Please, please don't go. I beg you, Mum, don't leave me. Just stay here. Please Mum, just stay here. I need you.'

At this stage, my mum would have been in a total panic, calling the doctor and the ambulance, and probably even the local priest for good measure. Luckily Veronica was made of tougher stuff. She just looked at her watch, and sighed, 'All right darling. I won't go anywhere. Jamie can stay home too. We can all just have a quiet day together. I'll just go and phone .... I mean I have to ... You see ...'

Alice and I looked at each other. We both knew who she needed to phone, but Veronica didn't know that we knew, so she couldn't tell us.

Veronica thought for a moment and then she spoke again in a rush. 'I'll just go and phone the crèche to tell them Jamie won't be in today.'

She went out, and I saw her taking the portable phone into her bedroom. She closed the door firmly behind her. A few minutes later she came back. 'That's it. All appointments cancelled. It's just us for the rest of the day.'

She looked kind of disappointed, and for one small moment I felt sorry for her. Maybe it wasn't her fault that she couldn't be happy with her husband. Maybe Norman was the first real love of her life. Maybe they deserved to be together. Maybe I was helping to ruin the best romance in the history of the world.

Then I looked at Alice, all miserable, curled up in her bed, still whimpering softly. Then I heard Jamie shrieking in the kitchen, and slamming doors loudly. I looked at the photograph of Alice's dad that she kept in a frame beside her bed. And I decided....

Well, I'm not quite sure what I decided – it was all too complicated for me. But I had a horrible day, cooped up in the small apartment with a cross Alice who had to keep pretending to be sick, a horrible Jamie, and a bored Veronica.

I think it was the worst day of my life.

So far.

Chapter eleven

Next morning, Alice made me get up even earlier. I wasn't very happy about this. After all, I was supposed to be on my holidays. I was supposed to be allowed to sleep late. Alice ignored my arguments though. 'Come on, Meg.' she said. 'It's after eight o'clock. The day is half over.' She sounded exactly like my mum. I thought it wiser not to mention this.

I was dressed before I had the courage to ask the dreaded question. 'Tell me, Alice, why did you make me get up so early? What exactly are you planning?'

Once again, I wasn't sure I really wanted to know the answer to my question. I could have saved my breath though, as Alice wouldn't tell me anyway.

'I'll tell you later when we have more time. But now we just need to get to the shop quickly.'

'Why?'

'Duh! Because I need to buy something.'

'Well, double duh to you! What do you need to buy?'

'You'll see, I promise. Just come on. There's no time to waste.'

And so I obediently followed her down to the local shop. As soon as we got there, Alice started to examine the labels on all the sweet packets. I had to laugh. She was just like my mum. Aaaaagh! Maybe she was turning into my mum. What a horrible thought. It would make a good movie though – *The day my friend turned into my mum*. Then I decided not – it would be far too scary.

I watched Alice until it seemed like she had examined every sweet packet in the shop. 'What exactly are you doing? Looking for e-numbers?' I joked.

'Yes, actually, I am.'

This was getting just too crazy. I stepped between her and the counter. I folded my arms and tried to look tough. 'Come on, Al. This isn't fair. Cut the mystery stuff and tell me what's going on.'

She shrugged. 'OK, so. If that's what you want.'

I tried not to look too surprised – Alice didn't usually give in so easily. She pulled me into a corner, and whispered in my ear. The shop was empty except for the little old lady at the till, so the whispering was a bit dramatic, but I let that go.

'Well, you know how Jamie's a bit wild?'

I nodded. Actually, he was more than a bit wild, he was often completely out of control.

'Well, if you think he's bad normally, you should see him after he's eaten some of these additives. He goes totally loopy.'

I was beginning to get the picture. 'So you feed him a big load of sweets, and he goes loopy?'

She nodded. 'Yep. And the great thing is, it works really fast. If we get home and give them to him quickly, he'll be crazy by ten o'clock.'

'Yeah. But your mum will just take him to crèche and let them cope with him, won't she? And how will that help you?'

Alice shook her head. 'Trust me on this, Meg. I know what he's like. He'll be so bad that even Mum wouldn't bring him to crèche. She wouldn't dare. So she'll have to cancel her date again. Norman will be getting really fed up.'

And then I realised that I shouldn't be arguing about whether the plan would work or not – I should be making Alice see that it was just a really, really cruel thing to do. I could hardly believe what I was hearing. I'd been listening to my mum going on about additives all my life. I knew how dangerous they could be. How could Alice do this to her brother?

Alice held up two packets of brightly coloured sweets. 'Will we get red or orange? Come on, Meg, you choose.'

Suddenly I was really, really angry. This was wrong. This was cruel. It was unfair on Jamie. And it was unfair on me. If my parents ever got to hear that I had been part of this plan they'd ground me for about a hundred years. For my mum, giving Jamie sweets like that was almost as bad as poisoning the child. I had to stop Alice. I just had to.

Alice waved the sweets under my nose. 'Come on, Meg,' she said. 'Choose which ones we should buy.'

I stamped my foot. 'No way, Alice! No way! I'm not choosing. You can't do this to Jamie.

Even he doesn't deserve this.'

Alice kind of stepped backwards in surprise. She wasn't used to me disagreeing with her. 'But–'

I continued. 'This is a crazy plan, Alice. This is even crazier than what we did at Halloween. We'll both end up in loads of trouble. And it won't even work. It couldn't work. Why don't you forget about Norman? Maybe your mum will fall out of love with him. Or he might fall out of love with her. You don't have to get involved. I think that sometimes it's best just to stand back and wait to see what happens.'

Alice was looking at me strangely, but she didn't say anything.

I still kept talking. This was turning into the longest speech of my life. 'Come on, Al. Put down the sweets.' (I felt like a cop on a tv show trying to make the bad guy drop his gun. Would it sound too weird if I said 'step away from the sweets'?)

Alice still said nothing, so I continued. 'Please, Al, let's go back to your place and have some breakfast. Let's have a good day together. Let's do some of the fun stuff you promised.'

'Megan ...'

I was glad that she'd said something at last, but her voice was quiet, and kind of scary. I was expecting her to be really angry with me, but she wasn't. She said 'Megan ...' again, and then she put her head down and started to cry. I'm not talking small little whimpers here, I'm talking huge, loud sobs. The woman behind the counter gave us a funny kind of look, but then she went back to reading the paper. After a few seconds Alice looked up. Huge fat tears were rolling down her face and onto the front of her jumper. She grabbed my arm which was still sore from the day before. 'Please, Megan, help me,' she sobbed. 'I'm not stupid, I know it's a really mean thing to do, but I have to do it. I just have to. And it's not only for me. It's for Jamie too. And Mum.

And Dad. Everyone will be better off as soon as Norman is gone from our lives. I'm doing this to save our family. And you've got to help me. Please, Meg. Please.'

What could I say to all that? I'd never seen Alice so upset before. All her toughness and her bravery seemed to have vanished. She just looked like a very, very sad girl. It would have been cruel to abandon her.

And, right at the back of my mind, I had a horrible feeling that if I walked away now, I'd lose my best friend forever.

And so, I very quietly said, 'OK, let's do it.'

I couldn't bear to choose which sweets to buy, so Alice ended up buying both the red and the orange packets. She handed them to the old lady behind the till. The old lady smiled at her. 'Don't eat all those at once young lady, or you'll be jumping around the garden.'

Alice smiled sweetly back at her, like the angelic child she wasn't, and we set off for home.

Veronica was up when we got back. 'Well. Alice,' she said, 'I'm glad to see that you're feeling better this morning. Where have you been?'

Alice smiled. 'I'm much better today, thanks Mum. I needed some exercise after spending all yesterday lying around, so Megan and I just went for a little walk.'

Veronica gave her a strange look. 'Well, that's a first. Now will you two go down to Jamie's room and get him up for his breakfast?'

Alice grinned. 'We'd just love to, wouldn't we, Megan?'

I nodded slowly and followed her to Jamie's room. Alice closed the door behind us, and went and shook Jamie gently. He sat up and rubbed his eyes. 'Go 'way, Alice. Freako.' He went to hit her, but Alice jumped out of his way. She turned to me with a smile. 'Years of practice.'

I didn't smile. Jamie was being horrible as usual, but he didn't deserve what was about to happen to him. But I was afraid to upset Alice again, so I just sat on the end of Jamie's bed, and watched.

Alice reached into her pocket and took out the two packets of sweets we'd just bought. Jamie's eyes lit up. 'Can I have one?'

Alice grinned. 'Of course you can. You can have lots and lots, ...'

Jamie reached towards one packet, but she took his hand and held it tightly, '...but first you must promise never ever to tell Mummy that I gave you sweets. OK?'

He nodded. 'OK!' He was so mad to get at the sweets that I knew he would have promised anything at all. Alice kept holding his hand. 'If you tell, I'm taking all of your bunnies and throwing them into the river. OK?'

He nodded. 'I promise. I won't tell Mummy.'

'Ever?'

He shook his head solemnly. 'Never, ever, ever.'

Alice smiled at him. 'That's my best little

brother. Now what would you like first? Red or orange?'

Ten minutes later Jamie had eaten most of the sweets. The only tell-tale signs were a few trails of red and orange down Jamie's chin. Alice licked a tissue (gross), and wiped the sticky mess from his face and hands. Then she helped him to get dressed.

We watched as he went off into the kitchen. Alice giggled and checked her watch. 'Now all we have to do is wait.'

'How long?'

She grinned. 'Not long at all.'

Chapter twelve

Alice and I had a quick breakfast, and then she seemed kind of keen to hang around at the table. I wasn't letting that happen though – I *so* did not want to be in the kitchen watching the countdown to Jamie's explosion. So I suggested that we go back into the bedroom for a while. Alice had to agree – if she had argued, it would have made Veronica suspicious.

We played *Don't Panic* for a while. Alice left

the bedroom door open, so we could hear what was going on in the kitchen. At first it was hard to notice any difference. Jamie was wild and bold, and completely horrible, but no more so than usual. For a while, I was able to hope that Alice's plan wasn't working. Maybe she had chosen sweets with natural colours by mistake. Or maybe Jamie was only affected by green sweets, or blue ones. Maybe this was going to be a normal day after all.

Soon I relaxed a bit, and concentrated on the game. I was better at it than Alice, but she never seemed to mind that I always won. She's generous like that. I raced into the lead, and was actually beginning to enjoy myself, when I noticed that, out in the kitchen, Jamie's behaviour was getting worse and worse. His voice was getting louder, his crying was becoming more frequent, and his mum was becoming more and more angry.

By ten o'clock Jamie was practically leaping

around the house. It was scary. Alice and I had abandoned the game. It was too hard to concentrate with the noise coming from the kitchen. We sat side by side on her bed, and listened. I could see our reflections in the dressing-table mirror. I looked like I had seen a ghost. Alice looked like she'd just won the lottery.

A while later, Veronica came into Alice's room. She looked tired and worried. 'What on earth is wrong with Jamie today? He's completely out of control. Have you any idea what's happened to him?'

Alice shrugged, and looked out the window. 'Was there a full moon last night?'

Veronica gave her a cross look. 'Very funny indeed, Alice. Now be serious. What will I do? I'm at my wit's end, and I'm supposed to be going out.'

As she spoke, Jamie came galloping along the hall, screeching and waving his arms. 'I'm a plane. I'm a plane. Look at me. I'm the biggest and loudest plane in the whole world.' He stopped for a second, took a deep breath, and let out a scream that made my ears ring.

Veronica grabbed his arm, and held it tight. Still Jamie jumped up and down waving his free hand in the air, narrowly missing her face. Veronica looked as if she'd like to hit him. Maybe if I hadn't been there she would have. She bravely put her face near his. 'You're not a plane. Do you understand? You're a little boy, though I have to say you're acting like a little baby this morning.'

At this, Jamie pulled free of her grip, and threw himself onto his hands and knees. 'I'm a baby. I'm a baby. Look at me. I have a big stinky brown poo in my nappy. Waaah! Waaah!' He crawled quickly along the hall and into the kitchen where his high-pitched screams continued. There was a loud clatter of pots and pans, a brief silence, and then more screaming.

I suddenly felt very bad. Alice was the one who had bought the sweets, and fed them to Jamie, but I had watched her do it. I was guilty too. I should have made her stop. I should have told Veronica what she was doing. Alice would probably never have spoken to me again, but even so, maybe it would have been the right thing to do. But there was no point in owning up now. The damage was done. I'd just have to sit tight and wait for Jamie to calm down.

Veronica sat on Alice's bed and put her head in her hands. 'What on earth will I do with him?'

Alice smiled sweetly. 'Send him to crèche?'

She was getting brave. But then, even I could see that Jamie couldn't possibly go to crèche while he was wound up like that.

Veronica could see that too. 'How can I send him to crèche? He's already on a warning, since he bit that little boy last week. And they've never quite forgiven him for killing Robbie Williams.'

I looked at Alice in horror. Jamie was bad, but surely he wasn't quite that bad. She grinned at me, and whispered, 'Don't worry. Robbie

Williams was the goldfish. Jamie flushed him down the toilet.'

Veronica gave her another cross look. 'It was an accident! And the crèche people blew it completely out of proportion. But still, if I send Jamie while he's like this he'll surely be expelled, and then what will we do? No other crèche will take him if he gets a bad name, and then I won't have a hope of getting him into a decent school in September.'

Alice smiled helpfully. 'You'll have to keep him at home today then, won't you?'

Veronica looked like she wanted to cry. 'I know. But I need to go out. I have to go out. Oh, Alice, what will I do?'

Once again I felt sorry for Veronica, but Alice just shrugged. 'How'm I supposed to know? Why don't you ask Dad? Oh, I forgot, you can't. He doesn't live with us any more. Silly me.'

I gasped at how cheeky she was being, but Veronica acted as if she hadn't even heard.

She suddenly brightened. 'Alice, would you be a pet and mind Jamie for me? Just for an hour?'

Alice shook her head. 'Sorry, Mum. If the crèche can't cope with him, how do you expect me to? After all, I'm only twelve. I'd like to help you, but I can't.'

I felt awful. Part of me wanted to offer to help Veronica, but the other part of me knew that if I did, Alice would never speak to me again. That was too high a price to pay – especially now that the real damage had been done. So I bit my lip and said nothing.

Veronica looked at Alice sadly, 'Alice what if ...?' she began, and then she stopped. I was glad. I knew that whatever it was that Veronica wanted, Alice would for sure say no. Veronica gave a small little sigh. 'Never mind. Do you think you could keep Jamie quiet for five minutes while I make a phone call?'

Alice didn't answer, so Veronica took her opportunity, and ran into her bedroom to make her call.

And so I found myself in the middle of my mid-term break, stuck in a tiny apartment, with the mother whispering into the telephone, the son rolling on the floor screeching and kicking and throwing saucepan lids, and the daughter secretly shoving more additive-laden sweets into his mouth, just in case the effects wore off too soon.

It rained for the rest of the day – heavy rain that beat off the windows, and then poured down the glass like someone was spraying it with a hose-pipe. The four of us clattered around the apartment getting on each others' nerves. I wanted to go out and do something, anything, but Alice just wanted to stay in her room – so that's what we did. We played *Don't Panic* about a hundred times, but it wasn't any fun. Alice was very quiet – I think even she was a bit shocked about how crazy Jamie went after eating the red and orange sweets. (Not shocked enough to stop feeding them to him though.)

The high point of the day was when we had chips and pizza for tea (again). That wasn't much good, because by then I was far too tired to enjoy them. I was glad when bedtime came – I needed some rest and relaxation. I lay in bed and closed my eyes and tried not to think about the day I'd just had.

Alice was still my best friend. That would never change. But I was beginning to think that if she succeeded in scaring Norman away from this family, she'd be doing him a very big favour.

Chapter thirteen

When I woke up in the morning, Alice was sitting up in bed watching me.

'Hi, Meg,' she said.

'Hi, Al,' I said.

I was too afraid to say any more. I didn't want to mention Jamie or Veronica or sweets or Norman or anything to do with the day before.

After a long time Alice spoke again. 'Know what, Meg? I think we deserve a day off.'

I hardly dared to hope. 'You mean ... a day with no secret plans?'

She laughed. 'Yeah, why not? I know you haven't had a very nice time here so far, and it's all my fault.'

'But what about–'

She didn't let me finish. 'I'll worry about Mum and Norman tomorrow. Today it's just going to be fun and games.'

A huge grin spread over my face. I didn't know what to say.

Alice laughed at my reaction. 'So what'll we do? You can decide.'

It didn't take me long to make up my mind, and in minutes our plans were made. We were going to go to the local cinema; there was a new film I *really* wanted to see. Then we were going to go down to the shopping centre for the super-frothy hot chocolate with marshmallows that I had been dreaming of for days.

I jumped out of bed, and got dressed in my best clothes. I was *soooo* excited at the thought of a normal fun day.

At about half past ten, Veronica had Jamie ready to go to crèche. He was pale and tired-looking. He hadn't calmed down until very late the night before. When I had been trying to get to sleep, I'd still been able to hear him jumping up and down on his bed and making train noises. And now he looked really bad. His skin was so pale it was almost blue, and he had huge black circles under his eyes – just like a baby panda. He was unnaturally quiet too. And while I was glad of that, it made me a little bit uneasy. It was as if Alice had really poisoned him, and I had helped her.

Veronica was quiet too. I felt a bit sorry for her. Her family was a total mess, and even though it was all her fault, maybe there wasn't anything she could do about it now. She didn't even ask us what we planned to do for the day. She just told us to be good (fat chance of that with Alice around), and then she set off for crèche with Jamie.

Alice and I went back in to her bedroom and listened to music for a while. We both knew that Veronica was probably going to meet Norman, so I kept chattering madly, trying to distract Alice. She was great though, she didn't mention Norman once. She just kept talking about the fantastic afternoon we were going to have.

At last it was twelve o'clock, and time to set off. I was all jumpy and giggly, like I usually get when I'm excited. Alice was excited too. She was really funny, telling me loads of great stories about her school and her crazy teacher.

It was only a short walk from the apartment to the Cineplex, and we were soon there. I stood outside the building and gave a big long happy sigh. At long last my real holiday was beginning!

Chapter fourteen

When we got inside the Cineplex, Alice was really generous and bought me a super-giant-sized tub of popcorn. I can never resist popcorn, and I was already half-way through it while we were still in the queue for tickets. Alice laughed when she noticed this. She put on my mother's voice, 'Megan Sheehan, do you have any idea how much salt you have just consumed?'

I giggled. Alice was a really great mimic, and if I closed my eyes it was almost as if Mum was standing in front of me.

Alice giggled too. She loves an audience. She continued, 'And do you have any idea how many trees are murdered every year to provide cardboard for cartons like that?'

I laughed again, and Alice launched in to a big speech about the environment. But after a few seconds I stopped listening, because just as she was getting warmed up, I looked over her shoulder and saw something that almost made me choke on my salty, environmentally-unfriendly popcorn.

It was something so bad that I could hardly believe it was true. I closed my eyes and opened them again, hoping that I'd been mistaken. But no, sadly, there was no mistake. I really had seen the most awful thing ever – because there, ten metres away from where I was standing, just near the front of the queue were ...... Veronica and Norman.

Alice hadn't seen them, and she chattered away happily, waving her arms in the air, having great fun mocking my mum's way of speaking. I tried to smile and act like nothing strange was happening – not easy when your very worst nightmare has just come true in front of your eyes.

The queue edged forwards slowly. Just a minute more, and Veronica and Norman would be buying their tickets. If only I could stop Alice from seeing them, they'd go to their film, and everything would be OK. Alice need never know that they were there. (They were hardly going to see the same movie as us.)

I kept smiling at Alice and saying things like 'Really?' and 'Wow' and 'You're so funny.' And I very nearly got away with it, but just as Veronica stepped towards the ticket desk, something made Alice turn around, and she gave a small cry of surprise. She grabbed my aching arm, and said, 'Oh, no! I don't believe it.'

I rubbed my arm and pretended nothing was wrong. 'Come on, Al,' I said. 'You're great at doing my mum. Say something else, or do Melissa!'

Alice ignored me. 'Look, Meg,' she hissed. 'Look over there.'

Of course I didn't need to look, but I did anyway. Veronica had just taken her tickets and she and Norman were walking towards the barrier. Alice raced after her. My heart sank. I'd witnessed lots of rows between Alice and her mother, and I knew they could get very loud and very messy. And this was a very public place for an O'Rourke special. To my relief though, Alice just stopped at the barrier and watched them walk away from her. Then she raced back to me.

'Change of plan. We need to go to screen six. I have to keep an eye on Mum.'

I felt like crying. 'But what about our film?

What about our fun day? You promised, Al, remember?'

Alice was decent enough to look guilty. 'I know, Meg, I did promise, but this is an emergency. My mother is going on a date. She's going to the pictures with a man who's not my dad. I can't just pretend it isn't happening. I can't go off and watch a film like everything's OK. I just can't.'

At least this time I could see how she felt. If I saw my mum going to the pictures with a man who wasn't my dad, I think I'd get a bit upset too.

We got to the top of the queue and Alice smiled at the lady behind the counter and said, 'Two tickets for screen six, please.'

The lady smiled back at her. 'And how old are you, young lady?'

Oh, no. We'd never checked to see what film was on in screen six. If it was G-rated, I don't think the lady would have been asking Alice her age. Alice smiled her best smile and crossed her fingers behind her back. 'I'm fifteen.'

The lady shook her head. 'I'm sorry, young lady, but I don't believe you. Screen six is showing a fim that's rated 15A. If you don't have proof of your age, you need to go in with an adult.' She smiled kindly. 'Is your mum around? Or your dad?'

I sighed. How could Alice answer that? '*Well, my dad's in Limerick, and my mum's just gone into screen six with her secret boyfriend. We're following her to see what she gets up to.*'

Alice looked at me, as if she could see what I was thinking. She leaned towards the glass partition that stood between her and the lady. 'My mum and dad are at work,' she said, 'But they know I'm going to that film. They said it's OK, honestly! They're cool about that kind of thing.'

The lady smiled. 'I'm sure they are, but if one of your parents isn't here with you, I can't sell you a ticket for screen six.'

Alice leaned towards her. 'Please. Pleeeease. You don't understand. It's an emergency. I just *have* to see that film.'

The lady shook her head. 'I'm sorry, love, maybe in a few years time. For now, why don't you go to screen four? There's a twelves film showing there. Just right for a girl your age.'

Alice didn't reply. She stepped away from the ticket-window, and went to sit on the floor near the barrier. After a moment, I went and sat beside her. There was no point staying in the queue. I knew there was no way Alice would want to see a film now.

'Now what?' I asked.

Alice shrugged. 'We wait.'

'For what?'

She gave an even bigger shrug. 'I don't know really. I just feel I should sit here and wait until Mum comes out.'

'Are you going to confront her?'

To my great relief Alice shook her head. 'No. That wouldn't change anything. I just want to see what happens, that's all.'

And so we waited. Ninety-seven minutes might not seem long when you're watching a really great film, but it seems very long indeed when you're sitting in the lobby of a cinema with your best friend who keeps saying things like 'How could Mum do this to us?' and 'I wish Norman would die of some horrible disease.' and 'I bet they're snogging.'

Every now and then Alice got up and paced around the lobby with a really cross look on her face. (She reminded me of the tigers in Dublin zoo.) Then she'd come back and sit down next to me again, and imagine out loud what was happening inside the cinema. She said a lot of very rude things about Norman, that I'm sure he didn't really deserve.

After what felt like about ten hours, the doors of screen six opened. Alice and I hid behind a cut-out poster for the next Harry Potter film. I wished I could be like Harry Potter. I wished I could wave all my problems away with one flick of a magic wand and a few made-up words. Why did real life have to be so complicated?

Just then, Veronica and Norman came out of the darkness, blinking the way you always do when you come out of the pictures. They walked towards the exit, and stood for a second, buttoning their coats and fixing their scarves. They were chatting and laughing. Veronica looked young and happy and carefree. She wasn't a bit like the cold, cross woman I usually saw. Maybe being with Norman really was good for her. Was it wrong for her to want to be happy?

I wondered if I should say this to Alice. Maybe I could persuade her to back off for a while. I looked at her, but she had a really cross expression on her face. Probably it wasn't a good time for this discussion.

I looked back towards the exit. Just then Norman leaned over and kissed Veronica on the cheek, and they walked off in different directions.

Alice didn't speak once on the way home.

It seemed like a very long walk.

*   *   *

Once again we hung around the apartment for the afternoon because Alice was too upset to go out.

Veronica didn't get back until tea-time. In one hand she had two fancy shopping bags. She was using the other hand to drag a cross-looking Jamie into the apartment.

Alice smiled at her, like she was really glad to see her. 'Did you have a nice day, Mum?'

Veronica sighed. 'It was just lovely until I went to pick up Jamie from crèche, and I heard how bold he's been. He bit one child and kicked another. And now he's banned from going any-where near Justin Timberlake.'

I had to interrupt. 'But how could he get near Justin Timberlake?'

Veronica shook her head impatiently. 'Easily. They keep him in the corner of the classroom, you know.'

What on earth was she talking about? Was everyone around here losing it?

Alice leaned over and whispered. 'She's not going mad. Justin Timberlake is the new goldfish. The replacement for Robbie Williams.'

I started to laugh but stopped quickly when I noticed that both Alice and her mother were giving me really cross looks.

Veronica continued. 'Jamie's on his very last chance in that crèche. The other parents are starting to complain about him. I don't know what I'm going to do with him, I really don't.'

Poor Jamie was probably still suffering from the after-effects of the sweets, and it wasn't fair to blame him. I decided to change the subject.

'You've been shopping Veronica. Did you buy anything nice?'

She smiled at me. 'Why, yes, Megan, I did actually. I got two nice new suits. Would you like to see them?'

'Yes, please,' I said.

'No, thanks,' said Alice at exactly the same moment.

Veronica gave her a funny look, then she said, 'Oh well, maybe later,' and she went into her bedroom with her bags.

While she was gone, Alice hissed in my ear. 'Don't show any interest. Don't go encouraging her. If she's buying fancy clothes for her special dates with Norman, I do *not* want anything to do with it.'

Just then Veronica came back out into the living room and sat down.

Alice put on her false-sweet voice again. 'Did you do anything else today Mum, besides shopping?'

I hardly dared to breathe. If Veronica lied, Alice would go ballistic, but she could hardly tell the truth either, could she?

Veronica was silent for a moment. Then she spoke quickly. 'Actually I went to the pictures.'

'Who did you go with?'

I held my breath again. How could Alice be so brave?

Once more Veronica seemed to think for ages before she answered. Then she said. 'I went on my own.'

Alice looked at me, and I looked at her. Of course we both knew her mother was lying.

Alice's voice was dangerously quiet. 'That's a bit freaky, isn't it?'

Veronica gave her a strange look, but didn't answer.

Alice spoke again. 'Going to the pictures on your own – how sad is that?'

She was taunting her mother, as if she was trying to force her to tell the truth. I didn't want to breathe, but I had to, I was starting to feel faint.

Veronica spoke softly. 'It was a film I really wanted to see. It was an inspirational film, all about a woman who faced terrible tragedy, but then turned her life around.'

Alice's voice was cold. 'What did she do? Did she leave her husband? Did she wreck her family?'

Veronica didn't even get cross with Alice. She just kept her voice calm. 'Don't talk about things you don't understand, Alice dear. Now if you'll excuse me, I think it's time I got the tea ready.'

She went into the kitchen and I was left with Alice. For the first time ever, Alice seemed to be lost for words.

After tea, Jamie went to bed, and Alice, Veronica and I watched reality TV for the evening. In the programme, a big group of crazy people were all living together in a small house. Any time they did anything strange, Alice said, 'That's so weird. Who'd really act like that?'

She didn't seem to expect an answer, which was just as well. What planet was she living on anyway? Had she *no* idea exactly how crazy her own life had become? Did she think that what was going on under her own roof was normal?

I sat squashed into a corner of the couch, and tried not to think too much.

*   *   *

Just before I went to bed, Veronica said that I could phone home. After Mum had gone through her thousand questions about my health and behaviour, we had a nice chat. She told me Rosie had learned to cycle my old bike with stabilisers. I really wished I had been there to see it. Then Dad came on and said he hoped I was having a lovely holiday, and I had to lie and say that everything was perfect, and that Alice and I were having the time of our lives.

Later on, when Alice was asleep, I cried for a long time. I wished I was at home. I wished I was back in Limerick with my own happy family. Being in Dublin with Alice was just too much hard work.

Chapter fifteen

When I woke up the next morning, I lay in bed with my eyes closed. I'd gone along with Alice's crazy plans so far, and I knew I wouldn't back out now. It was kind of like when you jump off a huge high diving board, there's no point changing your mind when you're half way down, and the water is rushing up to meet you. It was much too late for second thoughts.

I didn't even bother to hope that this would be

a normal day, and that we would actually get to do all the great things I'd been hoping for. I just lay there and waited to see what crazy stuff Alice had planned for the day.

After ages, I opened my eyes. Once again Alice was watching me from her bed. 'Hey, Meg, you're awake at last.'

I didn't answer. I was just too tired.

Alice sat up. 'Meg, I want to thank you.'

'For what?'

'For helping me the past few days.'

I shrugged. 'I didn't do much.'

'You've been here. And that's enough. I don't think I could go through this without you.'

Now why did that statement make me feel so guilty?

She continued. 'Really, you're being a great friend. And thanks to you, we're well on the way to getting rid of Nasty Norman.'

I smiled, but I wasn't convinced. If this Norman guy really loved Veronica, it wouldn't be that easy to shake him off. Two missed dates were hardly a catastrophe. And he'd looked happy enough at the pictures the day before.

As usual, Alice did her mindreading thing.

'We shouldn't have relaxed yesterday – that was a mistake. But we can make up for that today.'

I didn't mention that we'd only had about an hour of relaxation before we saw Veronica and Norman at the cinema.

Alice continued. 'Anyway, this is how things stand. Mum has missed two dates this week, and all because of her demanding children. Norman will be a bit fed up already, and today ... well today will be the icing on the cake.'

I got that sick feeling in my stomach that was becoming so familiar. I wanted to know, and yet I didn't want to know. I tried to keep the panic from my voice. 'Er, Alice, what exactly is going to happen today? Are you going to get appendicitis again? Please don't say you're going to give

Jamie more red sweets. I'm not having anything to do with it if you do. And I'm not going anywhere near the cinema after what happened yesterday.'

She smiled. 'Don't worry, it's none of those things.'

Whenever Alice said 'don't worry', I knew it was time to get very worried indeed.

'Don't worry,' she repeated. 'Today, we're trying something completely different.'

'Which is?'

'Today Norman is going to get to know the O'Rourke children.'

'And?'

She grinned. 'Well, it's too early to give you details. I haven't got the finer points worked out just yet. But he won't like what he sees – I can promise you that.'

* * *

Alice slipped into action during breakfast.

'Mum, Jamie looks really tired today,' she said,

'Maybe he shouldn't go to crèche.'

Veronica sighed. 'Yes, I know love, you're right. He does look tired. And after all the trouble he caused yesterday, it probably would be better to keep him at home, but I have to go out. I'll just send him in for a couple of hours.'

I looked at Jamie. His eyes filled with tears, which dripped down his cheeks and into his cereal. His bottom lip wobbled, and he used his two chubby fists to rub his eyes. I could see that the poor little pet still hadn't recovered from eating all those sweets. For the first time ever, I managed to forget all the times he'd kicked me and called me names, and felt really, really sorry for him.

Alice smiled at her mother. 'Poor Jamie. He's wrecked. Why don't you leave him here? Megan and I will mind him. Won't we, Meg?'

I nodded. There wasn't much else I could do, was there? I was on the roller-coaster and I didn't know how to get off.

Veronica didn't need to be told twice. She jumped up from the table, and kissed Alice's hair.

'Darling, that is so, so sweet of you. And you too, Megan. Thank you.'

I smiled, but I couldn't meet Veronica's eyes. If she knew exactly why her son was so tired, she wouldn't be thanking me, she'd be driving me to the railway station to buy a one way ticket for the next train home.

'I won't be gone long, I promise you. Just an hour or two. And you'll be good for the girls, won't you Jamie, love?'

Jamie nodded, and wiped away his tears, and Veronica hurried off into her bedroom to get ready for her hot date. Alice grinned at me, and gave me a thumbs-up sign. I smiled weakly back at her. I had a funny feeling that this was going to be the worst day of all.

Chapter sixteen

Veronica left the apartment a bit after half past ten, in a big cloud of happiness and expensive perfume. She sailed out the door like a prisoner who was being set free after serving twenty years in jail. I knew how she felt. I wouldn't have minded a break myself.

Fifteen minutes later, Alice, Jamie and I left.

Jamie was on his best behaviour. He held Alice's hand and skipped along beside her. After a while he gave her a cute little smile. 'Where are we going, Alice?'

'We're going for a nice walk.'

'Can I have sweeties again? Some of those nice red sweeties?'

I looked at Alice in horror. Surely she wasn't going to make him go loopy again?

She leaned over and whispered to me. 'Don't look so worried. Even I couldn't do that to him again. I'd be afraid he'd go so crazy that he'd never recover.'

Then she spoke louder to Jamie. 'No pet, no sweeties today. But if you're a good boy, we might find a nice coffee shop, and we can all go in and have some yummy hot chocolate.'

Jamie gave a little dance of joy. 'Yay! Yummy hot chocolate! Yay! Yay!'

Even though I love hot chocolate so much, I couldn't share in Jamie's happiness, because all at once Alice's secret plan had became crystal clear to me.

A few minutes later, we were strolling along the street where Veronica and Norman's 'usual place' was.

I had a few seconds to hope that maybe the chef had poisoned lots of people and that the place had been closed down.

Maybe there had been a fire during the night, and the whole place had been burnt to the ground.

Maybe there was a robbery going on, and the whole place would be surrounded by police.

But no. Unfortunately, the coffee shop door was half-open, and the sound of clattering cups and chattering people leaked out towards us.

Now my only hope was that Veronica and Norman wouldn't be in there – not a great hope, since they called it their 'usual place.'

I had to try one last time, before it was too late. I put my hand on Alice's shoulder, and stopped her for a second. 'Alice, are you quite, quite sure you want to do this?'

She thought for a moment. Then she spoke softly. 'Actually, now that you mention it, Meg, I don't want to do it.'

I breathed a huge sigh of relief, and then she continued, 'I don't want to do it at all. But I have to. I just have to. Please help me, Meg. Please.'

I could think of a hundred reasons to say no. I hesitated for a long time. In the end though, it was the usual choice – help Alice or lose her. So no choice really.

I shrugged. 'Come on. Let's go in and get this over with.'

Alice flashed me a quick smile of gratitude, and led the way inside.

Chapter seventeen

I saw them immediately. Veronica was sitting with her back to us, and Norman was facing us. They were leaning close together, with their heads almost, but not quite touching. He said something, and Veronica shook her head. Her lovely blonde hair slid softly along the back of her pale pink jacket. He said something else, and once more she shook her head. Once more her hair looked like a silky curtain, as it swayed gently from side to side. She looked as if she should be in a shampoo ad. I wished she was, instead of sitting there in front of me, not knowing that something dreadful was about to happen.

Then Norman reached over and put his hand on Veronica's arm. He smiled at her. He had lovely bright white teeth. If they got married they could make a fortune – he could star in toothpaste ads while Veronica advertised shampoo. I held my breath, afraid of what was going to happen next. If there was going to be another kiss, I totally did not want to be there to see it.

Maybe Alice felt the same. She grabbed Jamie by the arm and pulled him forwards. 'Look, Jamie, I think that's Mummy over there. Isn't that a nice surprise? Let's go over and say hello.'

Poor Jamie smiled his innocent little five-year-old's smile, and walked towards his mother. Alice followed him. I lingered by a nearby table and hoped that they'd be so surprised to see each other, that no-one would notice me.

Norman looked up as they approached, and then looked away again. He looked happy, but only because he didn't know what was about to happen. Veronica turned her head slightly, and then a look of surprise and horror flitted over her face.

'Alice, Jamie, what on earth are you doing here? Is there something wrong?'

Alice smiled a smile that was almost as innocent as Jamie's. 'Nothing's wrong. Megan and I just decided to bring Jamie out for a little walk, and he was so good, we said we'd buy him a cup of hot chocolate. So here we are. It's such a surprise to see *you* here.'

Veronica nodded absently. I could see that it was a surprise for her too, and not a pleasant one.

She looked for a long time at her daughter and son. Maybe she hoped that if she stared at them for long enough, they'd vanish into a puff of smoke. Then she spoke again. 'Where's Megan got to?'

I tried to sort of casually hide behind a pot plant. I *sooo* did not want to be there. I *sooo* did not want Veronica to see me.

Alice turned around. She saw me immediately of course – the pot plant wasn't all that big. She came towards me with a smile on her face. 'Silly Megan, what are you doing over here on your own? Come and join us. Look, Mum's here.'

I hissed at her. 'I'm fine here. You don't need me now. Leave me alone and just get on with whatever crazy stuff you want to do.'

I was trying to be loyal to Alice, honestly I was, but right then I was so afraid I could hardly think.

Veronica looked up. 'Oh there you are, Megan,' she said. 'Well you might as well come on over, now that Alice and Jamie are here.'

As she spoke she clicked her fingers like she was calling a dog. People were starting to give us funny looks. I didn't move. Now embarrassment was taking over from fear.

Veronica clicked her fingers again. 'For goodness sake, child. Come on over, and stop loitering there like a waste of space.'

I could feel my face go red. I didn't like her speaking to me like that, but I was too afraid to ignore her. I walked slowly over to the table and stood there with my hands in my pockets.

Norman had taken his hand from Veronica's arm, and was watching the scene with a half-smile on his lips. Poor thing. He had no idea what he was in for. Of course, I was with him in that, I had no idea what was going to happen either, but I knew it was not going to be nice.

There were two empty chairs at the table. Alice pushed Jamie and me into them, and then pulled over a chair from another table, and sat down herself.

Veronica was looking rather pale and tense. If

she hadn't been so rude to me I might even have felt sorry for her.

'Alice, dear,' she said. 'Maybe you should all just run along. I'll see you at home soon.' She rummaged in her purse. 'Here's some money. Why don't you stop and rent a DVD on your way home?'

Alice just smiled some more. 'That's very kind of you, Mum, but no thanks. That would be rude, wouldn't it? – going away when we've just got here. And since we're here, why don't we stay and have a nice cup of hot chocolate with you.'

Veronica put on a really cross face, though she was careful not to raise her voice. 'Didn't you hear me, Alice? I said–'

Just then Norman interrupted. 'It's fine Veronica. Let them stay.'

He looked at us each in turn and smiled. 'You must be Alice. Veronica has told me a lot about you. And this must be Jamie. And you must be Alice's friend from Limerick.'

Alice glared at him. Jamie ignored him. I tried to make up for them both by smiling the best smile I could manage, considering that what I really wanted to do was run away and hide under the furthest table.

Norman continued. 'I'm Norman, Veronica's ...', he stopped, and looked towards Veronica who shook her head slightly, 'I'm Veronica's friend.'

He smiled again. He didn't seem to notice that Alice was staring at him as if she would love to punch him really hard, right between the eyes. It was her 'tough-girl' look – I'd seen her practise it in front of the mirror once, when she thought I wasn't looking. Now I felt really sorry for the poor man. If he was going to hang around with the O'Rourke family for long, he'd better get used to that look.

Norman stood up. 'Now, I'm sure all these young people are hungry and thirsty after their walk. Hot chocolate and buns everyone?'

Jamie and I nodded. Alice continued to glare at Norman. I wanted to make her stop but I didn't know how. He seemed nice. If Alice had to have a stepfather, she could have done a lot worse than him.

Norman went up to the counter, and Veronica leaned across the table towards Alice. 'Come on, spit it out. What's all this about?' she hissed.

Alice shrugged, and opened her eyes wide. 'All what? We just happened to come along here, and you just happened to be here, and we met you, and now we're going to have a nice cup of hot chocolate together. What's wrong with that?'

Veronica's eyes narrowed. 'Nothing, I suppose. Just drink up quickly and get out of here. This isn't appropriate.'

Jamie looked up. 'What's "apopiate" mean?'

Veronica thought for a moment. 'It means you should be at home playing with your Lego.'

Alice stared at her mother. 'Why isn't it

appropriate?'

'It just isn't,' snapped Veronica. 'Now, I'm warning you, Alice. Behave yourself.'

Alice smiled sweetly at her. 'Don't worry, Mum you know you can rely on me.'

Just then, Norman came back with a tray full of drinks and buns. I could see the hot chocolate steaming. I could see the marshmallows already beginning to melt in the hot, milky foam. At last I was getting the hot frothy drink that Alice had been promising me all week. I should have been happy. But how could I be? I knew that the real trouble was just about to begin.

Chapter eighteen

Norman sat down and shared out the food. He'd bought everyone a hot drink, and there were about three sticky, creamy buns each. My mother would've had a heart attack if she'd seen so much sweet food piled up in front of me. Jamie's eyes opened wide, and he gave Norman a huge grin. Norman had won him over immediately. Norman turned to Alice. 'Won't you have a bun? They look delicious!'

She smiled at him, and I wondered if she too was falling for his charm. Then she reached into her mouth and pulled out a long stretch of bubble gum. Just when I thought it was going to break, she stopped pulling, and wrapped it round and round her finger. (I know it's gross, but I do that sometimes, but only when I'm on my own. I would never, ever do it in a crowded coffee shop.) Veronica glared at her. 'Alice, that is disgusting. Stop it at once.'

Alice smiled. 'OK, Mum. You're the boss.'

She unwound the gum from her finger, and popped it back into her mouth. Then she proceeded to blow the biggest bubble I'd ever seen. It hung from her face like a huge shiny pink balloon. Alice gave one last puff, and the bubble burst all over her face, making her look like someone who'd had a terrible accident. She grinned, and slowly began to peel it from her skin.

Veronica's face was red. 'Alice O'Rourke! Get rid of that gum. Now.'

'Whatever you say, Mother dearest.' Alice

rolled the gum into a ball, and stuck it to the underside of the table 'There. Now it's gone. Happy?'

Veronica gave her a vicious look. 'Yes.'

Alice smiled. 'Good. Now, don't let me forget it when I'm going. I've only had it for two days.'

She turned to Norman. 'Don't you just hate when you leave your gum behind somewhere when there's still hours of chewing left in it?' Norman gave a small chuckle, but stopped when he saw Veronica's face. He turned to Jamie. 'Well, young man, you'll have a bun, won't you?'

Jamie beamed at him, and took a bun, and tried to shove it into his mouth all at once. Even my little sister Rosie wouldn't have tried that. Sometimes Jamie seemed like the least mature five-year-old in the history of the world – maybe it was because of his mixed-up home life.

Anyway, he wasn't very successful in his efforts to eat the bun in one bite. Cream and crumbs tumbled from his lips and down all over his clothes. Veronica grabbed a serviette, and did her best to clean him up. As soon as she had finished, Jamie leaned over and took another bun. This quickly went the same way as the first one.

This was awful. I was out with the family from hell. I put my head down, sipped my hot chocolate, and tried to pretend I was somewhere else. Anywhere else in the world would have done – at home emptying the dishwasher, at the doctor's getting a verruca burned off, even school would have been better than this.

I looked up to see that Alice was scratching her head violently. Even though I was still scared and embarrassed, I had to smile. She certainly was inventive. Veronica was watching her, but saying nothing. Norman looked at Alice closely, and walked straight into her trap. 'Is there something wrong with your head?'

Alice shrugged. 'Nah. Not really. It's just lice. Jamie and I get them all the time. It's no biggie.'

Veronica leaned towards her. She spoke with her

teeth tightly clenched. 'Alice, I will deal with you later.'

Alice smiled at her. 'Thanks, Mum. But I think we're all out of lice lotion. Didn't we use the last bottle the other day?'

She turned towards Norman. 'We go through litres of that stuff. Mum ought to buy it by the bucketful.'

Norman leaned away from her with a look of distaste on his face. 'That must be very unpleasant.'

Alice shrugged. 'Nah, you get used to it. And it's not so bad. Least it's not as bad as the fleas. Anyway, me and Jamie are used to bad stuff like that. We're always sick, we are.'

Poor Norman edged his chair slightly away from her.

'I'm really sorry, Norman,' said Veronica. 'I can't think what's got into her. She's not usually like this.'

Alice gave a big loud laugh. 'Yeah, usually I'm

even worse. But luckily I took my medication before I came out.'

Now the people at the tables around us were beginning to stare again. I bet they were all planning to have great fun telling their families about the mad people they'd seen in the coffee shop. Norman was sitting slightly away from us with a puzzled expression on his face. Veronica was white-faced with anger, but I knew she couldn't do anything. She was probably afraid to correct Alice any more, in case it would make her behave even worse.

Just then Jamie reached out and took the last of the buns. While the rest of us had been watching Alice, he had managed to almost clear the plate. Even though it looked like half of each bun was still all over his face and clothes, that still left a lot of bun inside Jamie.

Veronica leaned over and stroked his head. 'Jamie, darling, maybe you've had enough of those buns. Why don't you put it back on the plate?'

Jamie looked at her for a moment, then he let out a huge loud wail, a Jamie special. 'Nooooo! I want the bun. I want it!'

Veronica spoke softly, even though she had a desperate look on her face. 'Why don't we wrap it up in a nice clean serviette and you can have it later?'

'*Noooooooooooo*!'

This time the wail was even louder and longer. The people at the other side of the room were now staring. I'd have been staring too, if I hadn't been stuck right in the middle of this awful scene. I looked at Alice. She was grinning like she was having the best time ever. She leaned over and whispered in my ear. 'Good old Jamie. He doesn't even know we're trying to scare Norman away, but he's doing it anyway.'

I whispered back. 'Yeah. Great. I'm very happy for you. Can we go now? Surely you've frightened the poor man enough.'

She grinned. 'Soon. We'll go soon I promise.'

Jamie was still wailing, and grabbing for the bun, which Veronica had somehow managed to pull from his hand. I bet she was really sorry she hadn't let him have it, but now she probably didn't want to back down in front of Norman. Even though she'd left it about ten years too late, she was probably trying to look like Super-Mom who was in complete control of her children.

'Darling, I'm sorry, but you can't have it. You've had too much already. You don't want to be sick, do you?'

That was a mistake, because just as she said the words, Jamie gave a huge choking kind of cough, and threw up a big heap of buns, along with the Coco Pops he'd had for breakfast. It was revolting. Like something out of a really gross horror movie. The brown, slimy stuff streamed down his clothes and all over the table. Alice and I are experienced big sisters, we know the routine. We both jumped up and moved away to get out of the line of fire. Poor Norman wasn't so experienced. He actually moved closer. 'Poor little chappie, you–' he was saying, as Jamie gave another huge heave, and the rest of the contents of his stomach came up in a huge explosion, all over the front of Norman's suit.

Veronica grabbed a serviette and tried to wipe Norman's jacket. It was pathetic. It was like using a tissue to hold back a tidal wave. The smell now began to hit, and people all around us were getting up and leaving.

Veronica kept apologising.

'Norman, I'm so sorry. So very sorry.' Over and over again. Norman probably wasn't listening. He was too busy trying to stop the stream of vomit from going into his shoes.

Suddenly Veronica turned to Alice.

'You… You …'

She could probably have thought of lots of words to call her only daughter, but none that she felt like saying in front of Norman. 'Just take your brother home, and put him in the bath. I'll see you later.'

The way she spoke frightened the life out of me, but Alice was defiant to the end.

'Sure, Mum. Like I said already, you're the boss.'

Then she leaned across to the sick-free side of the table and rescued her gum from under it. 'Mustn't forget this, must I?'

Then before her mother could respond, she took Jamie by the arm, and we left the coffee shop. As we went, Jamie began to wail again. 'I'm being good, amn't I? Can I have that bun now?'

Chapter nineteen

We got some very strange looks on the way home. Alice was on a high, like someone who'd eaten too many of the wrong kind of additives. She was kind of skipping along, with a funny gleam in her eyes. I didn't want to talk to her. I didn't know what to say to her when she was like this. For the millionth time that week, I wished I was at home with Mum and Dad and Rosie. It might have been boring, but after all this excitement, boring would have been just fine with me.

Alice was dragging Jamie along beside her. He was still wailing, but more quietly now, as if his batteries were running down. Tears and snot were streaming down his face, and his clothes were still covered in vomit. I shuffled along behind them, not because I really wanted to, but because I couldn't think of anything else to do.

We stopped to cross a road, and a little old lady came over to us. 'What's going on here? What happened to this poor little boy?' she asked.

The poor lady probably thought we were kidnapping him. I wondered why anyone would choose to kidnap such a revolting creature, when there were so many nicer, cleaner children around.

Alice looked at the old lady fiercely and opened her mouth. Before she could say anything though, I elbowed her aside. We were in quite enough trouble already.

I smiled my best smile, the one adults usually

love. 'It's OK. Honest it is. He's her little brother. We were out with her mother and he got sick and she's asked us to take him home and give him a bath.'

I wasn't even telling a lie.

The little old lady still looked a bit doubtful. She stepped closer to Jamie. I wondered if she was old enough to have no sense of smell. I certainly couldn't have stood that close to him. She pointed to Alice, who was quiet for once. 'Is that your sister?'

Jamie nodded.

'Then why are you crying so?'

'Because I want another bun.'

I smiled at the old lady again.

She nodded. 'Hmm. Run along then. Have a nice day.'

We ran along, but I doubted very much if I was going to have a nice day.

*   *   *

At last we got back to the apartment. Alice ran inside and got a huge plastic bag, then she made Jamie take off his clothes in the hallway and put them into the bag. She tied the bag tightly and threw it into the kitchen. Then she took Jamie into the bathroom, and I could hear the bath running. I could hear the splashes as he climbed into the bath, still wailing softly. Alice came out into the hall. She opened a cupboard and took out a towel. She was just going back into the bathroom, when I put out my hand and stopped her.

I was really, really cross. I didn't want to fight with her. I don't like fights at all, and I especially don't like fights with Alice. This time though, she had gone too far. I had to say something. I just wasn't quite sure what that should be.

I thought for a while, and then I took a deep breath. 'Alice, erm….'

She looked at me crossly. 'What are you trying to say, Megan. I have to get back to Jamie.'

I took another big breath. 'How...how could you do that?'

She shrugged. 'Do what?'

'You know what.'

She shrugged again. 'I don't know what you're talking about.'

It was the shrugging that got to me. How could she be so calm, after all that had happened? I got really mad, and at last I knew exactly what I wanted to say, 'You're *so* horrible! You've been really, really mean to Jamie. You filled him with those awful sweets the other day, and now you've got him all sick and upset. It's cruel. You can't treat him like that.'

She folded her arms and stared at me. I could see that she was angry too. Suddenly I was afraid. Alice and I had never had a really serious fight like this before, mostly because I always backed down before it got this bad.

Alice was defiant. 'It's all in a good cause. Getting rid of Norman is for Jamie's good too. He'll thank me in the end. Everyone will thank me in the end. You just wait and see.'

I opened the bathroom door, and peeped in. 'Look, Al. Just look at him.'

Alice looked in. Jamie was sitting in the bath, clutching a small rubber dinosaur. He was still sobbing. He looked up at his sister and sobbed some more. I smiled at him.

'It's OK, Jamie. Everything's OK now.'

His sobbing lessened a bit. I closed the door again, and turned back to Alice. 'It's not fair. You *know* it's not fair.'

She shrugged again. 'What do you know? He's my brother, not yours. It's easy for you with your lovely mum and dad, and your cutie little sister, all living happily ever after in Limerick. Just tell me, Megan, what do *you* know?'

I spoke softly. 'I know that even if my parents split up, and I had to leave my home and all my friends, even then I would never treat Rosie like you've treated Jamie. He's only five, Alice. He's only a baby. Fight your own battles, if you have to, but leave him out of it.'

Alice gave me a fierce look. 'You know nothing, Megan Sheehan. Nothing at all. *I hate you!*'

Then she went into the bathroom and slammed the door behind her.

Chapter twenty

I started to cry. I couldn't help it. I ran into Alice's room and lay on her bed and sobbed until her pillow was soaking wet. Then I got up, took my rucksack from the wardrobe, and began to pack up my things. I could get a bus to the railway station, and catch the next train home. I wasn't very happy about wandering around Dublin on my own, but staying would have been even worse. I needed to get out of that place, and the sooner, the better.

Alice was my best friend, but loyalty can only go so far. I was out of my depth, and I knew it. I tiptoed into the hall. I didn't want to talk to Alice again. I wasn't sure I ever even wanted to see her again. I tried my best, but lately, when Alice was around, things were just too complicated.

I could leave a note in the kitchen. I could just say that I was homesick, and wanted to go home. It was only half the truth, but still it wasn't a lie. I wanted to be at home more than I had ever thought possible.

I sneaked down the hall, glad that the thick white carpet was muffling my footsteps. As I tip-toed past the bathroom, I heard Alice speaking softly to Jamie.

Gradually his wailing stopped. I could hear the gentle splashing of water, and Jamie's chuck-ling. Then I could hear Alice singing quietly. 'Lavender's Blue' – a song we used to sing to him when he was a tiny baby. I stood for a moment listening. I could hear Jamie's small voice joining in with Alice's not very good one.

Then the bathroom door opened. I pressed myself in behind it. Alice and Jamie came out of the bathroom. Jamie was all wrapped up in a fluffy blue towel. Alice took him into his room, and put him into his pyjamas. They came back into the hall and went into the living room. I peeped around the bathroom door, and watched as Alice made a bed of soft blankets for Jamie on the living room couch. She gave him his favourite bunny to cuddle. Then she put on a DVD. She even kissed him gently on his cheek. 'Good boy, Jamie. You just sit quietly and watch your DVD, and call me if you want anything.'

He smiled at her. 'OK, Allie.'

For once, he actually looked sweet and cute, as he lay back on his blankets and sucked his thumb.

Alice came out of the living room and back down the hall. She closed the bathroom door, leaving me feeling a bit stupid standing there with nothing to hide me. She looked at me for a minute, and then she gave me a hug.

'You were right, Meg. I *was* horrible to Jamie. I got so wrapped up in my own plans, I forgot how awful it would be for him. He doesn't deserve that. I'm going to try to make it up to him.'

I smiled, and tried to wipe away the tears that were starting again. 'I'm glad, Al. Really I am.'

Alice continued. 'And I'm really sorry for what I said to you before. I don't hate you. I could never hate you. You're the best friend any girl could ever have.'

Just then she saw my rucksack. 'What's that for? Are you leaving?'

I nodded.

Alice sighed. 'I don't blame you. If it was me, I'd have been gone ages ago. You've been great to stay so long.'

I pulled a tissue from my pocket. There were so many tears, there was no point pretending any more. I wiped my eyes. 'I'm sorry, Al. Really I am. I want to help you, but I don't know how. It's all too hard. I just ...'

Alice smiled, but I could see tears in her eyes too. 'It's OK, Meg. It's going to be OK. Don't worry about me.'

I tried to smile. 'You've probably succeeded in getting rid of Norman. He'll never stay around after today, but your mother's going to kill you.' She shrugged. 'Luckily Mum doesn't believe in corporal punishment, so how bad can it get? She'll ground me forever, and I'll sulk for a while and we'll all get over it in the end. Come on, I'll walk you to the bus stop.'

I picked up my rucksack, and followed her down the hall. 'What will you tell your mum? She'll wonder why I left.' Alice thought for a second. 'I'll just tell her you got a sudden attack of appendicitis.'

We both laughed then. A happy and sad kind of laugh that made me feel a small bit better.

Alice looked into the living room. 'Jamie, I'll be back in five minutes. Don't answer the door. I've got my key. OK?'

He looked up and nodded.

We went down the stairs, and out into the car park. Two girls our age were walking by. They were talking and laughing. Normal happy girls. I wanted to be like them. I wanted Alice to be like them.

Alice and I didn't talk. She led the way to the bus stop just across the road and checked the timetable. 'There's a bus to Heuston train station in ten minutes. And there are lots of trains in the afternoon. You'll be home in time for tea. Maybe you'll get lucky and it will be organic spinach soup!'

She turned away suddenly, but not quickly enough. I could see tears pouring down her face. She gave me another quick hug, but didn't look at me. 'Gotta go. Can't leave Jamie on his own for too long.'

Then she ran back across the road, and in

through the door of her apartment building.

I buttoned up my jacket. It was still cold. I checked my watch. Mum would be surprised to see me home so soon. I hoped she wouldn't ask too many awkward questions. I'd have to remember to buy Rosie some sweets when I got to the station. I'd make sure not to buy red or orange ones – just in case. Maybe Grace and Louise would go to the pictures with me the next day. We could see the film that I'd never got to see with Alice.

For a few minutes, I tried to think happy thoughts about home, but thoughts of Alice kept getting in the way. She was all messed up and unhappy, and now she was in huge trouble as well. What kind of a friend was I, if I gave up on her so easily?

I looked up, and saw the bus coming towards me. All I had to was hold up my hand, and it would stop, and take me away from this place. I could be home in a few hours.

Then I thought of Alice again. I might not be able to do much, but maybe just being with her would help.

The bus trundled past me. I picked up my rucksack, and crossed the road again. A woman was just coming out of the building, and she held the door open for me. I went inside and up the stairs. I tapped on the door of Alice's apartment. After a moment, the door opened, and Alice was there.

'I thought you were Mum,' she said.

I smiled. 'Can I come in?'

She smiled back. 'Megan, I will never, ever forget this.'

I grinned. 'I've a funny feeling I won't either,' I said.

Alice hugged me, and we went inside to wait for Veronica.

Chapter twenty-one

We didn't have to wait very long. Alice and I were just settling down in the living room with Jamie, when we heard the rattle of keys in the hallway. I felt a cold shiver run right through my body. My teeth suddenly had that horrible sensation they get when the teacher accidentally scrapes her nails on the blackboard. I was tempted to run and hide under Alice's bed, but then I figured that if I did that I might as well have got on the train to Limerick, so I bravely sat where I was.

The hall door opened slowly. I heard the clatter as Veronica put her keys on the hall table. I heard the cloakroom door open and close, and only then did the living room door open, and Veronica appear.

There was a long, long silence. It was like the climax of a horror movie – with the sound turned down. Veronica stood in the doorway and surveyed the room. She looked at me, then at Jamie and finally at Alice. She stayed looking at Alice for what felt like about twenty minutes. It was such a cold stare that I was sure Alice would vanish into a puff of smoke. Right then,

I'd have happily vanished into a puff of smoke myself. But Alice didn't even look scared. My brave, foolish friend stared right back at her mother. Even Jamie knew there was something wrong. He looked frightened and sat in silence, sucking his thumb vigorously.

Finally, when I thought that we were destined to stay like that forever, Veronica spoke. Her voice was quiet. Scarily quiet. 'What on *earth* was that all about?'

Alice kept her gaze steady. Now I knew how she won all our staring competitions at school. 'What was all what about?'

'That, that ... that complete exhibition of hooliganism in the coffee shop. That's what.' Veronica's voice was slightly less quiet now.

Alice shrugged. 'Oh, that. We just wanted to join you for a nice drink of hot chocolate. What's wrong with that?'

Veronica's eyes narrowed.

I looked at my hands – they were actually

shaking, and I had to sit on them to make them stop. But Alice still didn't seem to be afraid. Clearly she was even tougher than I thought.

'It's not my fault Jamie threw up,' she said, 'Even you couldn't blame me for that. Norman shouldn't have bought all those buns. It looks like he doesn't know much about children, does he?'

Veronica took one small step forward. I know that hitting children is wrong and illegal and all that, but even I could see how she might have been tempted to hit Alice at that moment. Alice was looking at her mother like she'd just read the *How to Drive your Mother Completely Crazy* textbook. I could see Veronica clenching her fists until the knuckles went white. Her lovely pointy nails must have been digging into her palms.

Was this all going to end in tears?

Or bloodshed?

Were we going to be on the news that evening?

I started saying my nine times tables in my

head, in an effort not to be part of what was going on around me. As usual, I got stuck on nine times eight. I went back to the beginning, but had only got as far as nine times six, when, to my huge relief, Veronica stepped back again. She unclenched her hands, fixed her hair, and took a deep breath.

'Alice O'Rourke, tell me what was going on. Now.' The quiet voice was back.

Alice just stared at her mother, twiddling her hair and saying nothing. I felt like going over and hitting her myself. The truth had to come out in the end, so what was the point of all this messing? It was only going to make things worse in the end. Suddenly Jamie started to cry, 'Alice doesn't want you to have a boyfriend,' he sobbed, 'She wanted to make him go away. She told Megan. I heard her. She said she would be so bad that your boyfriend would run away and never, ever come back. Ever.'

I sighed. Well at least that was out in the open.

The waiting was finally over. Now it was time for the really big explosion.

Alice's eyes flickered slightly, but her expression didn't change. I looked at Veronica. She had both hands over her mouth, so all I could see were her long red fingernails lurking dangerously around her eyes. If she moved suddenly she could poke an eye out by mistake. Then she leaned forwards, and her golden hair slipped over her face. A horrible grunting noise came out. Not the kind of noise I thought I would ever hear from the elegant Veronica. She didn't look up. Her voice sounded like she was sobbing, 'Alice, tell me that's not true. Please?'

Alice sat up. The sulky look was gone now. I could see that she was afraid. And if Alice was afraid, I knew it was time to be very afraid indeed. Veronica was always in control, and if that changed, anything could happen. I nudged Alice and whispered. 'Tell her, Al. Please. She knows anyway, and surely, things can't get any worse. Just be brave and tell her the truth.'

Alice got up and walked to the window, and looked out. She spoke with her back to the rest of us, in a dead, expressionless kind of voice. Like she'd been practising for a while. 'Sorry, Mum. What Jamie said is true. But don't be cross. I did it for the family. Not just for me. You don't need a boyfriend. You have Jamie and me. I had to get rid of Norman. I didn't have a choice. Can't you see? I did it for all of us.'

Veronica still had her head down. All I could see was her mane of beautiful hair, which was shaking slightly. She didn't answer. Now Alice got really cross. She turned around and walked towards her mother. She caught her by both shoulders, and shouted. 'Mum, listen to me please. I did the right thing. I've saved this family. So don't be cross with me, please.'

At last, Veronica looked up. Her face was pale. Her lipstick was slightly smudged, and her mascara was smeared around her eyes making her look like an unusually pretty panda. 'Cross?' she said. 'I'm not cross.'

Alice stepped backwards. I could see that her anger had turned to fear again. She spoke softly. 'But I just scared away your boyfriend!'

Veronica took a deep breath. 'Why Alice darling, that is the funniest thing I've heard in years.'

And then the truth dawned on me. The wet streaks running down Veronica's face weren't from sadness or anger. They were tears of laughter. I hadn't heard anyone saying anything funny, but for some reason that I couldn't understand, Veronica was laughing at us.

Chapter twenty-two

Alice turned to me with a bewildered look on her face. I shook my head. I had no idea what was going on either. Maybe Veronica was losing her mind.

Should someone call a doctor?

Should that someone be me?

Every crisis needed someone sensible, and sadly, I couldn't see any other volunteers. I wondered if I should offer to make Veronica a cup of

hot, sweet tea, like they do in films, when someone is in shock.

Or should I slap Veronica in the face?

If I did would she ever forgive me?

Or would she slap me back? Now that really
would not have been fair.

Alice sat down on the couch, and looked on as
her mother slowly recovered herself. Jamie was
still sucking his thumb. He looked kind of
scared. I gave him a small smile as if to tell him
everything was going to be all right. I wished I
believed that.

Veronica gave one last laugh, and then she
pulled a tissue from her pocket and wiped her
eyes. She went and sat beside Alice, and put one
hand on her shoulder. Alice shook her mother's
hand off, and moved herself further along the
couch. Veronica spoke really quietly. So quietly
that I had to lean forward in order to hear her.
'Alice, darling. I think you've misunderstood.
You see Norman ...'

Alice interrupted her. Her voice was high and sharp. 'Oh, don't worry, Mum. I see all right. I see everything very clearly. More clearly than you know. I've heard you whispering on the phone to Norman every night. I've seen you getting all these new clothes and perfumes. I've seen your secret diary. I've even seen you meeting him in your "usual place". I've seen you kiss him. You don't have to tell me what to see.'

Veronica interrupted then. She looked as if she was going to laugh again. I started another round of nine times tables in my head.

'You've seen me kiss him? Kiss Norman?' Veronica was either genuinely very surprised, or she was a great actor.

Alice shrugged. 'Well, actually, it was Megan who saw that, but whatever? It was still a kiss.'

Veronica looked towards me. 'Megan?'

I shook my head miserably. I had stayed in Dublin to support Alice, but this was going too far. I wasn't going to get involved with whether or not Veronica had kissed Norman. It was all too crazy for me.

Alice rescued me. 'It was on Monday. You were in the coffee shop, and Norman arrived, and you kissed.'

Veronica smiled. Luckily she didn't ask how come we had seen her in the coffee shop on Monday. 'Actually you're right,' she said. 'Now that you mention it, we probably did kiss.'

Alice spoke in horror. 'You mean you're not even going to deny it?'

Veronica smiled a gentle kind of smile. 'Why deny it? It's true.'

Alice took a deep breath and opened her mouth, but no sound came out. She closed her mouth, and then opened it again. She reminded me of the goldfish I used to have, but that was a mean thought, so I tried to push it from my mind.

Then Veronica continued. 'Alice, please listen to me. I did kiss Norman, but it's not the way it looks. He's just that kind of a person. I've seen him kiss all kinds of people. It means nothing. It's just a social thing. To him it's just like a hand-shake. But anyway, that's not the point. The point is, Norman isn't my boyfriend, ...'

For a moment I wondered if he'd broken up with her because of Alice's behaviour. But Veron-ica seemed to have the same mind-reading skills as her daughter. She continued, '... he never was my boyfriend.'

Alice opened and closed her mouth a few more times, and eventually some words made their way out.

'Is that the truth?'

Her mother nodded. 'I wouldn't lie to you about something as serious as that.'

Alice made a puzzled face. 'But the phone calls, and the meetings, what were they all about?'

Veronica smiled at her, and once more she rested her hand on Alice's shoulder. This time Alice didn't shake it off. 'It was business. That's all. Norman has been helping me.'

Alice looked puzzled. 'Helping you with what?'

Veronica looked slightly uncomfortable. 'Well, he's ... he's ... . You see ...Well ...'

I'd never seen Veronica stuck for words before. Alice nudged her gently. 'He's *what*, Mum?'

Veronica sighed and answered quietly. 'Norman is my life coach.'

Chapter twenty-three

Now it was Alice's turn to laugh. 'I'm sorry, Mum, but that's soooo totally ridiculous. You don't need a life coach.'

Veronica smiled at her. 'Alice dear, life isn't always as simple as you see it. Adults sometimes ...'

She stopped and looked towards Jamie. He had actually managed to fall asleep in the middle of all the arguing. She got up, and covered him with a blanket, and tucked his bunny in next to him. Then she stroked his hair for a long time.

I turned to Alice. 'What on earth is a life coach?' I hissed.

Alice gave me a surprised look. 'Don't you watch any television? A life coach sorts out your life, if you're not smart enough to do it yourself.'

Veronica came over again. 'I heard that, young lady.'

She was smiling though, so I knew she didn't really mind. She sat down next to Alice. 'Like I said, life's not always as simple as you see it. And my life has been very difficult lately. I–'

Alice interrupted her. 'So? It's your own fault. You're the one who left Dad. You're the one who dragged us up here away from all our friends. You're the one who–'

She stopped and burst into huge, loud sobs.

'Oh, my poor baby,' Veronica said as she reached over and held her in her arms. She stroked her hair and rocked her, and said, 'There, there,' over and over again.

Alice cried and cried. I could see Veronica's pretty pink top becoming soaked with Alice's tears. She didn't seem to mind.

I was embarrassed. This was family stuff. I had no business there any more. Now that it looked like no-one was going to be murdered, it was probably safe to leave them alone.

I stood up, and tip-toed towards the door. Veronica waved me back to my seat. 'You might as well stay, Megan. You seem to be part of this.'

I *soooo* did not want to be part of it, but I didn't dare to disobey her. So I sat on a chair in the corner and pretended to read a glossy magazine while the O'Rourke family tried to sort out its problems.

It took ages for Alice to stop crying, but after a while, her sobs became less frequent and eventually they stopped altogether. Veronica continued to rock her for a while, and to murmur soothing noises, as if to a baby. Much, much later, Alice sat up and wiped her eyes. She was still holding one of Veronica's hands. I hadn't seen her do that since she was about five years old.

Veronica smiled at her. 'Will you listen to me for a while, and try to understand?'

Alice nodded.

Veronica took a deep breath and began. 'I'm afraid your father and I haven't been happy together for a very long time. It was all my fault. He loved me. You and Jamie loved me, and that should have been enough, but it never was. I spent hours at the hairdressers and the nail salon, and in the shops, but none of it made me happy. So I thought going away might make me happy and I decided to leave. But I never knew that it would hurt you and Jamie so much. I never knew you'd be so lonely, and so sad. I never knew that Jamie would be so upset and get so bold. And I never thought your dad would take it so hard. And I'm still bored and unhappy, but now everyone else is unhappy as well. Can you understand that?'

Alice nodded. 'But where does Norman fit into all of this?'

'Well, one of my friends told me about him. You're right – he helps silly people like me to sort out our lives. He gets me to think through my options, and decide what to do next. He gives me small tasks to do, like homework, and I have to keep a diary of all the things I'm good at.'

I couldn't help smiling to myself. Poor Alice thought her mum was keeping a diary of romantic dates, when all she was doing was homework for her life coach!

Veronica went on, 'And then he checks up to see how I did.'

Alice sat up straighter. 'So that's why you had to meet him every day?'

Veronica nodded. 'That's it. We'd meet, and we'd discuss what I would do. Once he sent me to work for an afternoon in a charity shop. He–'

Alice interrupted, 'And the trip to the cinema?'

I gasped. Veronica didn't know that we'd seen her at the cinema with Norman, and I'd been kind of hoping to keep it that way. Luckily Veronica didn't seem to notice Alice's slip.

She smiled. 'The trip to the cinema was another of Norman's tasks. Like I told you at the time, it was a film about a woman who managed to turn her life around. I told Norman that going to the pictures on my own was just too sad, and that's why he came with me. Mostly though, I just had to do stuff on my own.'

'What kind of stuff?' Alice actually sounded interested now.

'Well, another day I had to visit a museum and imagine what it would be like to work there. Once I had to try to go a whole day without shouting at you and Jamie.'

She gave a small smile. 'I failed that test I'm afraid.'

Alice grinned at her, and Veronica continued.

'Then in the evening—'

Alice interrupted again. 'Then in the evening, Norman rings you to see how good you've been.' Veronica nodded. 'That's it. That's why Norman has been phoning. I suppose I could have saved us all a lot of grief if I'd told you what I was doing, but I didn't quite know how to say it. I was afraid you'd think it was just too silly. So I said nothing. It seemed like a good idea at the time.'

She stopped talking then, and everyone was quiet for a while. I actually flicked through a few pages of my magazine. There were a few nice pictures of frilly tops. I wondered if there was any chance of persuading my mum to buy one of them.

Suddenly Alice started to giggle. 'Poor Norman. The gum, and the lice, and then Jamie throwing up. What on earth did he think?'

Veronica shrugged. 'He was very good about it actually. After a while he even began to see the funny side of it. Though of course we had no idea why you were behaving so badly.'

Alice covered her face. 'Oh, Mum. I'm so sorry. I was so cheeky to you.'

Veronica patted her knee. 'Well, I had told him that you and Jamie were ... um ... being ... how can I say it ... um ... a little bit difficult since we came to Dublin. At least he got to see that I was telling the truth.'

Alice looked at her mother. 'Mum, I'm really so sorry. And I've never really thought of you being unhappy. I never thought of your feelings. I always just blamed you for everything.'

'I'm sorry too. And I wish I could have been happy with your dad, but I couldn't. I'm sorry. But we'll get through this. I promise you. Things are bad now, but we'll get sorted out, I promise you that.'

Veronica leaned over and wrapped Alice in her arms, and they had a big long hug. I couldn't remember the last time I'd seen Alice hug her mother.

I smiled. I had a funny feeling that Veronica was telling the truth. Everything was going to be all right in the end – with or without Norman's help.

I didn't have to pretend to be reading any more. Jamie was still fast asleep, and as far as Alice and her mother were concerned, I might as well have been invisible. I got up and tip-toed to the door. I went into the kitchen, and helped myself to a big glass of fizzy orange, a huge packet of crisps and two chocolate biscuits.

I'd had a very long day, and it was the least I deserved.

Chapter twenty-four

I hung out in Alice's bedroom for a long time. No-one came looking for me, but I didn't mind about that. I was glad of the chance to chill out all on my own. I passed the time by listening to Alice's iPod, and reading all of her magazines.

Every now and then I could hear Alice and Veronica laughing. After a while, I heard Jamie joining in. The poor little boy had had a very tough time over the past few days, and I was glad he was happy. I began to hope that maybe Alice hadn't damaged him for life after all.

Listening to Jamie laughing made me a bit lonely for my own small sister, Rosie. I never thought I'd miss her – after all she's just a little kid. But I found myself really looking forward to seeing her again. I wanted to hear her saying 'Meggie' in that cute little way of hers. I wanted to sit down on the couch and bounce her on my knee, and sing 'Bobby Shaftoe' to her.

Even though things seemed to be all right again, I was glad that I was going home the next day. Six days in Dublin hadn't sounded like much when I'd planned it, but it had turned out to be a very long time indeed.

Much, much later, Alice came into the

bedroom. She was tired-looking, and a bit pale, but she was smiling. She sat on the bed beside me. We looked at each other.

'Well?' I said.

'Well what?'

'Well, I haven't seen you for a while. How are things?'

She grimaced. 'Oh, Meg. I'm sorry. I've left you on your own for ages.'

I grinned. 'That's OK. I needed the rest!'

She laughed. 'I can't bear to think about how wrong I was. How could I have been so stupid?'

'It's not your fault,' I said. 'Who ever would have thought that Norman would turn out to be a life coach? I didn't even know such a thing existed until today!'

Alice sighed. 'Maybe you're right. But I can't believe how stupidly I behaved this morning. Why didn't you stop me?'

I made a face at her, and she went on.

'OK, so you did try. As usual you were right,

but as usual I didn't listen to you.'

She gave a sudden giggle. 'I hope I never meet Norman again.'

I giggled too. 'Don't worry, I don't think he'd be in a big hurry to meet you again either.'

We were quiet for a while. Then Alice said, 'It seems crazy now, the idea of Norman being Mum's boyfriend.'

I thought that perhaps some day Veronica might have a boyfriend, and Alice would just have to get used to it. This wasn't the time to mention that though.

'So how's your mum now?' I asked.

'She's fine. We had a great chat. We sorted a lot of things out. For the first time in my life, I feel a bit sorry for her. And for the first time I was able to tell her how I feel without shouting at her. In the end I told her everything. I told her about the first day we followed her, and about the fake appendicitis, and about seeing her at the cinema.'

'And what about giving Jamie the red and orange sweets?'

Alice made a face. 'OK, so I told her almost everything. I think I'll save telling her about the sweets for another time.'

'And how is Jamie now?'

'Poor Jamie. He spent the last hour curled up in Mum's arms. He was really quiet and sweet. He'll probably be a brat again tomorrow, but we'll deal with that. From now on I'm going to help Mum with him though. Before, I kind of encouraged him to be bad, to punish Mum for bringing us here.'

I smiled. 'I'm glad it's OK.'

She lay back on the bed. 'Yeah, me too.'

I thought for a moment. 'You know, it's a bit like your last crazy plan.'

'How?'

'Well, last time, you wanted to make your mum move back to Limerick, and even though that didn't work, at least she ended up letting you visit more often. And this time, even though there was, in fact, no boyfriend, things seem to be better. You're able to talk to your mum anyway. I think you're all going to be happier now. So in a funny way your plan did work after all.'

She grinned. 'Maybe you're right. But, Meg, I'm sorry about all of this. You must have had a horrible few days.'

She was right. If I ever got to write my life story, this wouldn't really rate as the highlight of my existence.

I just shrugged though. 'Ah, you know. It was fine really.'

Alice looked closely at me. She knew I was lying, and I knew she knew. It didn't matter though. White lies are allowed between friends.

Alice jumped up. 'Anyway, put on your best clothes. Mum's taking us all out for something to eat.'

My best clothes weren't all that great. So I put

on my nicest pair of jeans, and Alice lent me a really cool top to go with them. Then we straightened our hair, and put on some of Alice's new perfume, and some pale pink nail varnish.

Veronica came in then.

'Wow, girls. You look great!' she said.

Alice gave a small mock bow. 'Thanks Mum. You don't look too bad yourself. Where are we going anyway?'

Veronica wrinkled up her face. 'I'm not sure really. There are so many nice places, it's hard to decide. Maybe I'd better ...'

Alice and I looked at each other, then we both shouted together ' ... consult your life coach.'

Then the three of us laughed until we felt sick.

Chapter twenty-five

Next morning I woke up feeling great. It was my last day in Dublin, and the first without one of Alice's secret plans. Our only plan that day was having fun.

At breakfast, everyone was on their best behaviour. Jamie ate his cereal nicely, and Alice and her mother chatted like they were the best friends in the whole world. I was almost jealous, except with Alice so happy, that would have been a bit mean.

As we were tidying up, Alice asked her mother, 'Are you meeting Norman today?'

Her mother gave a funny smile. 'Yes, I am. We don't finish our course until Friday of next week. You don't mind, do you?'

Alice laughed. 'No, Mum. Not at all. Would you like to leave Jamie with Megan and me?'

Veronica thought for a moment. 'It's nice of you to offer, but no thanks. He really needs to settle into a routine. It's best if he goes to crèche today.'

I looked at Jamie, expecting a tantrum, but he just grinned and said, 'Yay! I'm going to crèche. I'm going to play in the sand with Jake and Niall.'

I put my head down, trying to hide my smile, and wondered how a family could change so completely in twenty-four hours.

After Veronica and Jamie had left, Alice and I went down to the local shopping centre. I bought the sweets I'd promised Rosie – nice, safe, pale pink ones with all-natural colouring. Then we went to the 'design-a-teddy' shop. I made a really cute yellow teddy for Rosie with a big orange bow around his neck. Alice made Jamie a bright purple bunny with red ears. It looked just like the crazy kind of thing Jamie would love.

For Mum I got a bottle of organic shower gel. It was a horrible slimy green colour, and it didn't smell especially nice. Well, to be honest, it smelled fairly revolting – like nettles or rotting grass or something, but I knew it was just what she would like.

I got Dad a soccer magazine, and a bar of his favourite orange chocolate.

Alice and I chipped together for a really nice book for Jamie.

'He loves when I read to him, but I hardly ever do,' she said. 'I'm going to read to him every single night from now on.'

I smiled to myself again. I knew that half the time she'd be too busy doing other stuff, but it was nice that she thought she would.

After that we just hung out. We went up and down the glass lift until the security guard came and stopped us. He wasn't really cross though, he just winked and said maybe we'd like to give it a rest for a while. Then we got fruit smoothies (Mum would have been proud of me), and crisps. Next Alice made me stand outside a jewellery shop, and when she came out she had a small package wrapped in shiny purple paper. She tucked it into my jacket pocket with a stern warning. 'Don't open it until you're on the train.'

When we got back, it was time to pack my bag again, and Veronica drove us all to the station. Veronica bought me two magazines and a book. The others weren't allowed past the metal barrier, so we said our goodbyes there.

'We'll miss you, Megan,' said Veronica. She'd often said that to me, but for the first time ever, I felt that she really meant it. Jamie pulled my jacket until my ear was level with his mouth. 'I didn't tell Mummy about all the red sweeties. I promise.'

I grinned at him and whispered back, 'Good boy. I think that's best. It can be our little secret.'

Then he gave me a huge sloppy kiss on the cheek. I had to wait until he wasn't looking to wipe it away with the back of my hand. Alice gave me a hug. We never used to hug when we lived next door to each other. Now it seemed like we never did anything else.

'When will I see you?' I asked.

'Well, next weekend I've got a school concert, and Dad's coming up the weekend after that, so maybe the weekend after that?'

She looked at her mother, who smiled. 'That sounds fine. You can go to Limerick then.'

We all said one more goodbye, and then I went through the barrier and walked to the train. When I got to the step, I looked back. Alice was tickling Jamie, and Veronica was laughing at them both. They looked happier than I had seen them in months.

Alice looked up and waved. I waved back, and then I got onto the train.

As soon as I was settled in my seat, I opened the package Alice had given me. It was a tiny silver bus on a chain. It was sweet, but I wasn't quite sure why she was giving me a bus. Then I noticed a note tucked into the bottom of the box.

This is your own personal Life Coach.
Thanks for everything.
XXX Alice.

I laughed. Then I sat back in my seat as the train began to move. I closed my eyes. It seemed like I had been away for a very long time indeed.

I thought back to the journey to Dublin. I remembered Mum's note. I wondered just how many of her rules I had broken. Still, what she didn't know, couldn't hurt her, could it?

*   *   *

Much later, the train pulled into the station in Limerick. Mum and Dad and Rosie were on the platform waiting for me. I ran off the train, and hugged everyone. Then Rosie started jumping up and down and pulling my arm.

'Sweeties. Sweeties. Sweeties for Rosie?'

I smiled as I reached into my rucksack. It was great to be back.

And that, as they say, was that…

…except for one more thing.

Chapter twenty-six

On Saturday morning two weeks later, I was cleaning out my bedroom when the doorbell rang. I ran to answer it. I needed a break from sorting out piles of dirty odd socks and old copies and stuff.

I opened the door and there stood Alice with a huge smile on her face. At first I was too surprised to say anything. I just stood there with my mouth open. I probably looked a bit stupid, but Alice was kind enough not to point this out. Finally some words made it to my mouth.

'Al!' I said. 'What are you doing here? I thought your dad was going to Dublin to see you this weekend.'

She shrugged.

'Yeah, he was,' she said airily. 'But there's been a small change of plan. I came down here instead.'

I laughed. 'So I see. Come on in.'

I was delighted to see her. Hanging out with Alice was sooo much more fun than matching up old socks. (But then I suppose, most things in life are more fun than matching socks.)

Alice followed me into my room. There was something funny about her, but I couldn't quite make out what it was. She seemed strangely on edge. Kind of jumpy and nervous. And that made me nervous.

Questions raced through my mind.

Why was she here?

Why was she on her own?

Had she had a row with her mum?

Had she come to tell me about yet another crazy plan of hers?

Would I be strong enough to resist if she wanted me to help her out again?

She sat on the bed, and I sat next to her. Even though I had so many questions, I was afraid to address the real issue. I *sooo* did not want any more drama.

'Want to listen to some music?' I asked.

She shook her head.

'Play Monopoly?'

Another shake.

'Play Swingball?'

One more shake. I was running out of ideas. Alice had just said 'no' to all of her favourite things. What on earth was going on here?

She turned towards me. Her eyes were all kind

of sparkly.

'Go on, Meg. Ask me,' she said.

Now I was completely confused. 'Ask you what?'

'Ask me why there's been a change of plan. Ask me why I'm here.'

I sighed. 'OK. Why has there been a change of plan? Why aren't you in Dublin with your dad?'

She didn't answer. I felt like shaking her. 'Al, talk to me. Tell me why you're here.'

And then Alice jumped up and pulled me by the arms until I was standing up too, and she hugged me and danced up and down like someone who had completely lost her mind. I endured it for a minute, and then I pulled away. Extreme behaviour always makes me nervous.

'Al?' I said doubtfully. 'What's going on?'

She stopped dancing and spoke in a big confused rush. 'You see, I'm not in Dublin, because Mum wanted to come to Limerick for the weekend. She said we had to come. She's ... She's ...

426

she's looking at an apartment. We're ... We're ... I mean ... Mum and Jamie and me ... We're ... '

She stopped speaking and hugged me again, and I hardly dared to hope.

'You're ... ?'

She nodded.

'Yes, we're ...' It seemed like neither of us could say the words. There was a moment's silence, and then we both burst out together.

'We're moving back to Limerick!'

'You're moving back to Limerick?'

And then we both jumped up and down and screamed and hugged and then jumped up and down some more.

Ten minutes later, when we had calmed down a bit, Alice explained what had happened.

'Well, in the end we have Norman to thank,' she said.

'You mean it was his idea?'

Alice laughed. 'Not exactly. He's a life coach. He's not allowed to have ideas. He just listens until his clients have their own ideas.'

I laughed too. 'And?'

'Well, after four weeks of Norman's expensive time, Mum discovered that by moving to Dublin, all she'd done was bring her old problems with her, as well as creating a few new ones.'

'A few?'

She laughed. 'OK. So she created lots of new ones. Anyway, Norman helped her to see that living in Limerick wasn't the problem at all. And that running away to Dublin was only going to make things worse. So we're coming back. We'll be able to see Dad every day, and I can see you whenever I want. And Jamie can go back to his old crèche where he used to be so happy, and where no one knows what he did to Robbie Williams!'

I laughed, and she continued, 'Mum's going to do an interior design course, and then try to get a part-time job.'

I laughed. 'Good old Norman. I wonder

should you send him a thank you card?'

Alice shook her head. 'Don't think so. I don't think he'd want to be reminded of my existence.'

'I suppose you're right. Anyway, when are you moving back?'

'That's the best bit. Once Mum makes up her mind, she acts very quickly.'

That was true. One day last August Veronica decided to move to Dublin, and less than a week later they were packed up and gone.

'So how quickly?' I asked.

'As I said, she's looking at an apartment right now. It's just around the corner. Near the shop. If she likes it, we're moving back at Easter.'

I thought for a moment. 'But that's only three weeks away.'

Alice beamed at me. 'I know. Isn't it the best news ever? After Easter I could be back at school with you. We can do our homework together. We can hate Melissa again. We can make our confirmation together, just like we always planned.

Everything will be just like before.'

I smiled and repeated. 'Everything will be just like before.'

'Except Mum and Dad won't be fighting all the time.'

Alice was smiling so much I thought her face would split in two.

It mustn't be possible to die of happiness, because if it was, I'd have died that day. It looked as if we were going to live happily ever after, after all.

An hour later, Veronica called over with Jamie. Alice and I ran to meet her at the door. Veronica waved a set of keys in the air. 'Good news. It's ours for a year. To start with. We can move in whenever we like.'

Alice hugged her mum until she begged for mercy.

Mum brought Veronica in for a cup of herbal tea. We all sat together in the living room. Jamie played Barbies with Rosie. Alice and I did each